ANNIE MOUSE'S

FAMILY VACATION

Number 5.5 in The Adventures of Annie Mouse series

A companion to Annie Mouse's Route 66 Adventure: A Photo Journal

This book is dedicated to all of the Route 66 business owners and "Roadies," past and present, who keep the Spirit of 66 alive!

With special thanks to David P. Keppel for his tireless work on the design and layout of this book.

To the Reader

May you enjoy your "Kicks on 66!" For your reading pleasure, you may refer to the photographs found in Annie Mouse's Route 66 Adventure: A Photo Journal, available in print through www.anniemousebooks.com, and both print and Kindle e-book through Anne Slanina's author page on Amazon:

http://tinyurl.com/nagovqq

Each book can be enjoyed alone, but your reading pleasure can be enhanced by viewing the photographs in the Photo Journal while reading the chapter book.

Other Annie Mouse Adventures by Anne M. Slanina that you will enjoy include:

  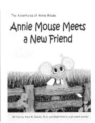  

All books available in print and as e-books.

ANNIE MOUSE'S

FAMILY VACATION

Number 5.5 in The Adventures of Annie Mouse series

ANNE MARO SLANINA

ILLUSTRATED BY KELSEY COLLINS

ANNIE MOUSE BOOKS, HARRISVILLE, PA

Library of Congress Control Number: 978-0-9914094-1-9
ISBN: 2014930136

Please note that the businesses along Route 66, as in all of the country, change constantly. Information was accurate at the time of publication. Please enjoy your trip along the Mother Road and always watch out for your own safety!

Annie Mouse Books
P.O. Box 142
Harrisville, PA 16038

www.anniemousebooks.com
anniemousebooks@yahoo.com

Table of Contents

Chapter One:
The Last Day of School

School had just let out and Annie Mouse hurried to the corner to meet her brothers and sisters as soon as the last bell rang. They couldn't wait to get home! That morning at breakfast Mommy and Daddy Mouse told Annie and her brothers and sisters that there would be a special surprise waiting for them when they got home from school.

Annie couldn't wait to find out what it was! She knew it would be a good surprise since she could tell Mommy was excited. It seemed like it took forever to get home! The whole way home they wondered what the surprise would be.

Annie kept trying to hurry the others along. "Can't you guys walk any faster? Don't you want to find out what the surprise is?"

Big brother Bobby told her to slow down. "If you're not careful, you're going to get hit by a car," he warned.

Big sister Jenny didn't seem to care to find out what the surprise would be. "Slow down, Annie! I'm sure the surprise isn't a big deal, anyway. I bet Mommy baked a cake for us. Big deal!"

Sam disagreed. "I know Mommy likes to make her special cakes for special occasions, but did you see how excited she looked?! I've never seen her act like that before. Annie's right- this is going to be a BIG surprise! I'm with you, Annie- let's hurry!"

"Slow down!" shouted the triplets, little sisters Sarah, Sandy and Sally, in unison. "We can't keep up with you!"

Annie slowed down and waited for them to catch up. "I just wish we still had a school bus. We would have been home by now!"

"Buster and Billy probably already know what the surprise is, anyway. They're lucky. They don't have to go to school yet. If it's a cake they probably already got into it and ruined it," whined Jenny. She never got excited about things the way Annie did.

Chapter Two:
The Big Surprise

Finally, they were home! Grandpa's old car that had been abandoned in their field was now parked beside their home. Annie was the first to reach the front door. She nearly knocked baby brothers, Buster and Billy, over as she burst into their home shouting, "Mommy, Daddy, we're home! Where's the surprise? What's the surprise?"

Annie looked around and noticed that many of their belongings were packed up. Suddenly she was afraid. Maybe this wasn't a good surprise, after all! What if they were moving! She wanted to cry. She loved their home now that she had a best friend, Molly Mole, who lived close by. She didn't want to move!

Jenny noticed the bags of clothes and food, too. "I told you it wouldn't be a great surprise, Annie. But I didn't think it would be a BAD surprise!"

Mommy and Daddy were kneeling on the floor, looking over a large map of The United States. "Are you ready to hear the surprise, kids?

Annie and her brothers and sisters rushed forward, almost knocking Mommy and Daddy over in their eagerness to get closer.

Finally, Daddy announced, "We're going on a vacation!"

"A VACATION," all the kids shouted together. They had never been on a vacation and weren't sure how they felt about it. They had heard other kids talk about vacations, but they had never been on one.

"Where?" Jenny asked. "I hope it's no place dumb."

"How? Are we FLYING? I'm afraid to fly," Annie said, while holding back tears.

The others chimed in with, "Why? How long will we be gone? Do we hafta go?" They were all shouting at once.

"Calm down! Quiet down! Everyone sit down on the floor around the map," Daddy ordered, while drawing a red line across the map.

Once they were settled, Daddy began explaining. "We've all had a rough couple of years. Billy's illness and heart surgery left us tired, but thankful to have our family together. Mommy and I thought it would be a great time to get away for a little while."

He continued, "You know Grandpa's old station wagon that's been sitting out in the field for years? Well, I've been working on it and finally got it running! I had always promised your mother that we would go on a trip out west so that she could visit her family in California, but we never made it. Now with the station wagon running, we could finally go!"

Annie asked, "What's the red line you drew on the map for, Daddy?"

"I was just getting to that," Daddy answered. "We'll be following

Route 66 as we travel west to California. The red line shows the historic route that goes from Chicago, Illinois to Santa Monica, California."

Annie couldn't believe that they would be traveling all across the United States!

The sound of the kitchen timer sent Mommy running. A few moments later she called them to the table, "Dinner's ready."

Daddy said, "Come on, kids. Let's go eat. We'll talk more about the trip over dinner."

Annie was excited to learn that she would finally be able to use her camera that she had received for her birthday and would be able to take her own photographs!

Jenny said it wasn't fair that Annie had a camera but no one else did. Mommy reminded Jenny that she could have asked for one for her birthday, but she chose to get a new bike instead. When Mommy turned away, Jenny stuck her tongue out at Annie. Annie just turned away. She wasn't going to let Jenny ruin her excitement.

Finally, Daddy told them, "Mommy and I are going to finish looking at the map to plan out our route while you kids get everything cleaned up and ready to go. We are going to leave tonight, as soon as everyone is finished with their chores and is ready to go."

"TONIGHT?!" the children all cried out at once.

Daddy explained, "Mommy and I are going to take turns driving through the night while you children sleep. We'll be driving the interstate through the night, so there won't be anything interesting to see until we get to Illinois in the morning."

As the children ran off to do their chores, Daddy began to spread out the map. Annie wished she could sit there with them and find out exactly where they were going. New adventures scared her and she didn't know what to think. But Annie had never seen her Daddy look this excited before. And Mommy was smiling, too. She looked really happy and she hardly ever yelled when Daddy was around. This might be fun!

Chapter Three:
The Adventure Begins

PENNSYLVANIA

Annie and Jenny went off to do the dishes. Throwing soap bubbles at Annie, Jenny said, "I don't know about this vacation thing. We're going to be squished in that stupid car all across the country."

Annie yelled, "STOP throwing soap at me, Jenny! You got some in my eyes!"

Daddy and Mommy came running into the kitchen to see bubbles everywhere! Mommy yelled, "I don't think these kids want to go on a vacation!"

Annie pointed to Jenny and cried, "I want to go- but not with HER."

Daddy scolded, "That's enough you two! I see it's time for a family meeting! Jenny, clean up this kitchen, now! Everyone else, I want you in the family room when your chores are done!"

A short while later, with chores done, the children quietly went into the family room. Daddy instructed them to sit down.

"If there is anyone who doesn't want to go on this trip, you can stay with your grandmother while we are gone. Jenny, should I call your grandmother?" Daddy asked.

"No, Daddy, Grandma will make me wash windows if you send me there to punish me! I'd rather go on vacation with you," Jenny replied in a panic.

"Okay then. I don't want any more trouble! We are going to be in the car for a very long time. You will all need to follow some rules while we are gone. I will not tolerate any whining or misbehaving from any of you. When we make a rest stop everyone must go to the bathroom. And most important of all, everyone must stay with Mommy or Daddy at all times! If there are any problems, I will turn the car around and we will go back home! Got it?" he asked.

In unison, the children all responded, "Yes, Daddy!"

"Okay then! Let's get going!"

As soon as Daddy finished talking, all of the children hurried outside, eager to ride in the car. Daddy followed them. But, WHERE WAS MOMMY?

Daddy looked back towards the house and saw Mommy with her hands on her hips, staring at them.

Daddy scowled, wondering what was wrong. Suddenly it hit him!

"Everyone, back to the house! Mommy has more bags and she needs help loading them," Daddy ordered.

When they got back to the house, Mommy scolded, "Even though we are going on a vacation, there is still work to be done, and I don't want to be the only one doing it! I wondered how long it would take you all to realize that you had forgotten our supplies."

Then she told them to use the bathroom "one last time" before picking up a bag and carrying it to the car.

One by one, each of the older children returned to the car carrying a bag. Daddy did a headcount to make sure everyone was there.

Finally, with everything packed, the children began to pile back into the car. Sam and Bobby said since they were the oldest they got to pick the back seat that faced backwards.

Jenny whined, "I want to ride in the back seat!"

Annie said she just wanted a window seat and didn't care which back seat she was in.

Daddy reminded them that he would not tolerate any fussing. "From now on, I'll tell everyone where to sit and everyone will have a turn to sit in the back seat at some point. We'll be in the car a long time!"

As Daddy and Mommy began strapping the twins into their car seats, Daddy instructed everyone where to sit. While Annie was waiting for her turn to get into the car, she realized she didn't have her camera! She had put it down on a bench by the door when she went back to help Mommy with the bags. She quickly ran back to the house, grabbed her camera, and started to run back to the car.

Annie could not believe what she was seeing! The car was moving slowly down the driveway! They were leaving without her! She started to run after the car, yelling, "Hey, wait for me!"

At about the same time, Bobby had just noticed that Annie's seat was empty and yelled to the front, "DADDY, DADDY! Wait! We don't have Annie!

Daddy slammed on the brakes. Everyone saw Annie running behind the car at the same time. Sam opened the back door and Annie jumped in. "I can't believe you were going to leave without me," she cried.

Jenny, Bobby, and Sam all started to laugh. Sometimes Daddy liked to joke with them. Annie thought maybe this was one of those times. Still out of breath, she gasped, "Daddy, were you playing a trick on me or were you really going to leave me?"

Daddy responded sternly, "I wasn't teasing you. Why didn't you get into the car? I did the headcount and you were right there! I thought you were already in the car."

Annie quickly explained what happened. "You should have told me you were going back to the house, Annie," Daddy scolded. "Make sure you tell someone where you will be at all times. Since there are so many of us, it's easy to get lost."

Annie apologized to Daddy and said it wouldn't happen again.

Finally, with everyone in the car, the BIG ADVENTURE was

about to begin. Annie began to giggle with excitement. She had never been on such an adventure before! She wondered where their first stop would be and how long it would be before they stopped.

Mommy suggested that they all just curl up and go to sleep. They never went to sleep this early and Annie wondered how anyone could sleep when they were THIS excited, even if it WAS their bedtime!

Knowing that they were not ready to sleep, Daddy asked if they would like to hear a little bit about the places they would be visiting. Annie wondered if Daddy was about to tell them a story.

A story from Daddy was a rare treat! Daddy was always so busy he hardly ever had time to sit and tell stories, but when he did, they were wonderful. This trip was already fun! As they quieted down, he began to tell them about traveling in the old days.

Daddy began, "Once, a long time ago, there were no highways that went all across the country the way they do now. When people would head out west, they had to take many smaller roads that went through a lot of small towns. The roads were marked Route 66 and you knew that if you were heading west, you just kept following the signs for Route 66. It took several weeks to travel across the country because the old roads weren't paved like today's highways and they were very difficult to travel. The cars weren't built to go fast like they do today, either. Cars would break down or get flat tires. If it rained a lot, the roads would get muddy and cars would get stuck in the mud. Families would have to stay in towns while their cars were repaired or the weather got better. The people along those roads built a lot of businesses for the travelers. There were diners, motels, camp grounds, gift shops, amusement parks and lots of other fun things for families to see and do as they made their way across the country."

Daddy continued, "When the modern highways were built they bypassed many of the smaller towns. Travelers were able to drive straight through without even stopping in towns. People didn't need so many hotels and restaurants once they could get across the country quickly. Many of the towns that relied on Route 66 travelers are empty or almost empty now. Since Mommy and I aren't used to driving in the busy traffic of the interstates, I thought it would be fun to take Route 66 to California and get a chance to experience it first-hand."

As Daddy turned onto Interstate 80 westbound Annie asked, "Is this Route 66, Daddy?"

Daddy replied, "No, Annie, this is Interstate 80. Traffic moves much more quickly on I-80 than it does on Route 66. The new highways are for getting someplace quickly. Since we are eager to explore Route 66, I want to get there quickly. We'll take things a lot slower once we get on Route 66."

Sam said he had heard about some of this in his Social Studies class and he couldn't wait to be able to tell the kids at school that he had actually traveled on Route 66.

Jenny yawned and asked when they would get to do something exciting. She didn't understand why anyone cared about roads; they all looked the same to her.

Annie just glared at her big sister and told Daddy that SHE was interested in his story.

Daddy continued, "Since Route 66 doesn't begin until Chicago, we will have to take the interstate through Pennsylvania, Ohio, and Indiana. That's one reason why we are driving through the night; I hope the interstate traffic isn't as bad as it is during the day. The Illinois Route 66 Visitor's Center is in Joliet, just south of Chicago, and that's where we will begin our Route 66 adventure. We should arrive in Joliet tomorrow morning."

Annie asked, "How do you know so much about Route 66, Daddy?"

Daddy explained that when Mommy's relatives, Cousins Mary and Bob, moved to Needles, California from Pennsylvania they traveled parts of the historic route and told Mommy and Daddy all about it.

"I'm not sure what else we will see before we get to California, but when we get to Arizona, we'll stop at the Grand Canyon, before we continue to California," Daddy concluded.

"THE GRAND CANYON?!" they all shouted at once. Even Jenny was excited now! This kept getting better and better!

Chapter Four:
Annie Gets Sick

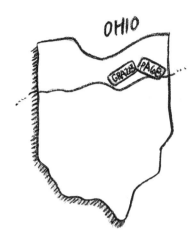

No one felt like sleeping after they heard that they would see the Grand Canyon. Once Daddy's story was finished, Annie and her brothers and sisters talked excitedly about their adventure. They had all heard about the Grand Canyon in school and had seen pictures. It seemed ENORMOUS!

Daddy warned them that it would take several days to get there and they would have many adventures before arriving in Arizona, The Grand Canyon State. He was just as excited as they were, but he knew that since they would be doing a lot of interstate driving before they reached Illinois, there would be miles and miles to go before they would see anything exciting.

It wasn't long before they saw a sign that welcomed them to Ohio. Wow, they were already in another state! Annie had never been out of Pennsylvania before! They had rarely gone anywhere other than the area surrounding their farm near Slippery Rock. Daddy laughed as he explained that they'd only been driving for 45 minutes!

Bobby thought it might be fun if they started to play a game. "Let's see how many different states we see on the license plates of the cars that go by." They had already seen Pennsylvania and Ohio, so Bobby said those didn't count.

Mommy and Daddy were thankful that the children found something to do to occupy their time as the miles rolled by.

"I just found Michigan," Annie yelled.

Sam said he found Ontario and wanted to know if that counted, since it wasn't a state. They all decided it counted, since it was not a Pennsylvania license plate.

Jenny said she found one, but didn't know how to say it. She spelled, "M-I-S-S-O-U-R-I" and asked, "What state is THAT?"

Daddy helped them by saying it was Missouri, and added that it was one of the Route 66 states that they would be going through, right after Illinois.

Annie continued to wonder where their first stop would be. She couldn't see much of anything except grass and trees. The land was flat and the scenery didn't seem to change much. It made her realize how much she liked the mountains and hills where she lived.

"Mommy, I'm hungry," Annie called to the front of the car. "Do we have any snacks?"

Daddy said he would stop at the next rest stop so they could all get a snack, stretch their legs and go to the bathroom.

"Oh good! I'm ready to begin exploring!" Annie exclaimed.

Daddy explained that it would just be a quick stop. He reminded them that it would be awhile before they stopped for sightseeing.

Disappointed, Annie slumped back into her seat. The children continued to stare out the window looking for new license plates. Cars and trucks were passing by their station wagon so fast that Annie started to get dizzy watching them. Daddy, who wasn't used to driving, was going much slower than most of the other cars on the road.

Daddy saw the sign for the next rest stop at about the same time as the triplets began to fuss. Sarah was the first to start to yell, "I have to go to the bathroom!" Immediately, the other two chimed in. No matter what, the three girls always acted as a unit!

Daddy told them to hold on; they would be there in a few minutes. Annie started to cry, too. "Daddy, I think I'm going to throw up! I don't feel so good."

Mommy quickly handed a plastic bag back to Annie and told her to use that. It was a good thing, too, because before Daddy had a chance to stop the car, Annie proved that she did, indeed have to throw up!

The bigger kids all started to yell and began rolling down all of the car windows. The car didn't smell very good at all!

Jenny asked, "Couldn't you wait to do THAT?"

Annie started to cry harder. Mommy said, "Thank heaven we were planning on stopping for a little break anyway!"

Daddy pulled into the parking lot. He opened the car doors and all the kids jumped out as quickly as they could, eager to get away from the smell! They all waited outside the car while Mommy took care of Annie.

Mommy pulled the crying Annie to her lap and felt her forehead. "You don't feel warm. I don't think you have a fever, Annie. I wonder what's wrong."

Annie explained that she had been watching the cars and trucks go by and just felt dizzy all of a sudden. Mommy then understood what had happened.

"Annie, when I was a little girl, I went on a long car trip with my family once. I got sick like this, too. It's called carsickness. Some people get it when they look out the side windows and see everything go by so quickly that it makes them feel dizzy. You'll feel better in a little bit. Make sure you only look out the front window from now on."

"Let's get into the restroom to get you cleaned up and then we'll sit outside for a little bit while the car airs out," Mommy suggested.

To Daddy, she said, "I think Annie just needs some fresh air. It's just a case of carsickness."

Mommy told all the girls to come with her and the boys to go with Daddy. She did not want anyone to be in a bathroom alone. Annie was glad since she had never seen a public rest stop before and felt uncomfortable with all those strangers in the bathroom. Their house had a nice, homey smell about it, but this rest room smelled funny and she didn't like it. No one wanted to stay in there very long! They didn't waste any time doing what they needed to and getting out of there!

Back at the car, Mommy pulled out some crackers and a bag of cheese from their cooler and suggested that they eat at a picnic table for a few minutes. After finishing their snack, no one was ready to get back in the car.

Daddy walked back to the car and pulled something out from under the seat. He held up a football and pointed to a grassy area behind the picnic tables and asked, "Who wants to play with me, over there?"

The bigger kids all went running and soon they were laughing and giggling and trying to tackle Daddy for the ball. Daddy always knew how to have fun with them!

Annie just watched them play while she ate her crackers; she still felt a little queasy. Mommy sat with her while the babies crawled in the grass.

All of a sudden the sky got dark and storm clouds were rolling in. Everyone went running back to the car just as the rain started to pour down.

Daddy laughed, "Well, that's the weather in Ohio - sunny one minute and storming the next!" They were all giggling as they piled back into the car.

Mommy said it was her turn to drive and Daddy should rest awhile. Bobby wanted to continue playing the license plate game, so the children began to stare out the window in search of different states. Annie said she was done playing THAT game for now! Soon it was too dark to see them easily and the others quickly lost interest, too.

It was now long past their usual bed time. The noise from the back seats began to subside as the children began to get drowsy.

Even though Annie was determined to stay awake so she could experience every moment of the trip, she soon felt her eyes getting heavier and heavier as the station wagon rolled along at a steady pace. Soon she and the other children were all fast asleep.

Mommy smiled as she realized her entire family was asleep around her and she found that she enjoyed the rare silence. She was beginning to think this was one of Daddy's best ideas ever!

Chapter Five:
The Flea Market

INDIANA

ILLINOIS

Mommy and Daddy continued to take turns driving through the night while the children slept. They had traveled through the Ohio and Indiana turnpikes and were now entering Illinois with Daddy driving.

The sun was beginning to rise and Mommy and Daddy talked about the day's plans while the children slept. The traffic was getting heavier and heavier and Daddy wasn't sure which lane he should be in to go to Joliet.

Mommy said with all the big trucks passing them, she couldn't see the signs ahead. By the time Daddy could tell which lane he should be in, it was too late; he was in the wrong lane when the interstate split. Daddy couldn't get over in time and was off the planned route.

Daddy told Mommy to look at the map and see where they were going. "Well, what should we do now?" Daddy asked.

Mommy was looking at the map and trying to figure out where they were headed. She told Daddy they could continue along this route and they would start their Route 66 adventure closer to Chicago than they originally planned, but that just meant they'd be seeing more of Route 66.

Daddy said he didn't mind that adventure, as long as he didn't get stuck in Chicago traffic. He admitted he was a little nervous driving in the big city.

Suddenly, Mommy saw a big sign for a flea market, and said, "That might be a fun place to stop. I saw this place in one of the Route 66 travel guides. We could probably get some breakfast there and look around a little before continuing to the Joliet Route 66 Visitor's Center."

Daddy said he remembered seeing it in the travel guide, too, but it seemed so huge they could probably spend the entire day there! Mommy and Daddy both agreed it would be a good stop, but just for a little while.

Annie woke up before the rest of the kids and had been listening to Mommy and Daddy talk. She wanted to see if she could hear what plans her parents had before the rest of the children knew about them. Her brothers and sisters were still sleeping as Daddy began to slow down to take the exit ramp.

As the station wagon pulled into the parking lot, the rest of the children began to wake up.

"Where are we?" Bobby asked while rubbing his eyes.

The rest of the children were soon excitedly chiming in with the same question.

"Are we ready to see something exciting?" Jenny asked.

Mommy pointed to some big signs that announced the flea market and said, "We're going to make this our first adventure."

"Daddy, THEY'RE SELLING FLEAS THERE!!!!" all the children screamed at once.

Daddy and Mommy laughed at the children's confusion. They had heard of a flea market before, but had never actually gone to one. While Daddy parked the car, he told them they would soon see what a flea market was. The children quickly scrambled out of the car.

Upon walking into the flea market area, they saw ... STUFF. All kinds of stuff. There were toys and furniture and tools and kitchen appliances and clothes. They even saw animals in cages and fruits and vegetables with signs on them. But no fleas anywhere.

Daddy found a table with disposable cameras and other camera supplies. He thought it might be a good idea to get one for each of the older children so they could all take their own special pictures, not just Annie. Mommy agreed that it was a great idea. Daddy said Annie could have an extra storage chip for her camera. Annie was excited to learn that she would be able to take as many pictures as she wanted throughout the trip with the new chip.

Chapter Six:
Annie Gets Lost

The Mouse family continued to walk down a big aisle towards an area that sold cheese. Mommy thought it would be good for breakfast.

Along the way, Mommy and Daddy got distracted looking at canning jars and tools. These things didn't interest Annie at all and she became impatient waiting for Mommy and Daddy to continue down the aisle!

Suddenly, she spotted a big ball. It was the biggest ball she had ever seen. It was close to where Mommy and Daddy were, so she thought it would be okay to wander over to check it out. She was only gone a second, but when she looked up, Mommy and Daddy were nowhere in sight!

Annie thought she saw Mommy up ahead and hurried to catch up to her. WHEW, what a relief! She wasn't lost after all.

She continued to follow behind, trying to catch up to Mommy and determined not to get lost again, but where was the rest of the family?

"Mommy slow down," she called. The woman didn't even turn around!

"MOMMY?" she shouted again after the woman.

When the woman turned Annie realized that it wasn't Mommy

she was following after all! She WAS lost! Now what would she do? There was no sign of her family anywhere!

Annie began to cry. She remembered what Daddy had said about making certain to stay together. She wondered if any of them even noticed that she was missing. What if they had already left? What if she would never see her family again? She wanted to scream, but she was so afraid that when she opened her mouth, nothing came out.

Which way should she look? She wished she hadn't stopped to look at that ball. How had she managed to lose her entire family??!! It was so hard to see where she was going with tears in her eyes. If she ever found them again, she would NEVER, EVER let her attention wander again. By this time, she was crying so hard a few people began to notice her and stopped to ask her questions. This only scared her more.

"What's wrong little girl?"

"Did you lose your mommy?"

"What's your name?"

Annie tried to talk but could only gulp and sob.

Meanwhile, Mommy and Daddy were frantically looking all over for Annie. They had been at the cheese counter asking all of the children what kind of cheese they would like, when they noticed Annie was gone.

Sam thought they should all split up and look for Annie in different directions. But Daddy insisted that all of the other children stay right with them, since they couldn't have more children getting lost.

Mommy and Daddy were scared. There were so many people around and Annie was so little. How did they lose her?

"Annie, Annie, where are you?" they all hollered together.

Mommy started to cry. "I hope no one took her, where could she have gone, I only turned my back for a second."

Just then, Daddy saw a small group of people gathered in a circle. "Look, over there," he pointed to the gathering. "Those people all look concerned. Maybe Annie is over there."

They all rushed over, pushing through the crowd of people, and there Annie was, sobbing, on the floor, still clutching her camera.

Daddy was the first to reach Annie. He picked her up and hugged her. Mommy was crying and kissing her at the same time. Then, Daddy and Mommy scolded her for wandering away from them, "Don't ever leave us like that again! We were so frightened that we had lost you for good!"

Annie was so excited to see her family. She promised she would never wander away again.

Jenny wasn't about to let Annie off so easily, "How could you get lost like that? What's wrong with you?"

Daddy said sternly, "Let's just get back to the car. Follow me." He began walking quickly in silence.

No one, not even Mommy, said anything after that, they just followed Daddy.

It seemed like an awfully long walk back to the car. Annie couldn't be more miserable. No one was saying anything. What if Daddy and Mommy were so upset they decided not to go to the Grand Canyon, after all? It would all be her fault if they never saw the Grand Canyon. Her brothers and sisters would surely hate her forever if that happened.

Chapter Seven:
A Long First Day

They were all out of breath by the time they got back to the station wagon. Huffing and puffing, they all piled back into the car. Now that the crisis was over, Daddy and Mommy reminded everyone of the rules, and how important it was that no one leave the group again. Since Annie was still crying, they knew she was very sorry and no one said anything else to her about it.

Annie, still sobbing, said she wasn't ever leaving the car again, not even when they got to the Grand Canyon! Then, she curled up into her spot and cried herself to sleep.

The whole family was exhausted from the experience. Mommy was afraid Daddy blamed her for losing sight of Annie, the older brothers were afraid they would be in trouble for not looking after their little sister and Daddy was tired from having been so scared. He had never been around that many people before. That was scary enough, but he had never been as frightened as he was when he realized that Annie was lost among all of those people!

The Mouse family rode on in complete silence as the station wagon rumbled along. Mommy was still holding the bag of cheese she had bought for their breakfast, but she had no appetite now. The older children were too afraid to mention they were still hungry.

Finally, Daddy laughed and said, "I guess we forgot about our breakfast," as he heard some rumbling coming from the twins' tummies.

"It won't be long before we'll be in Joliet," Daddy said.

He asked Mommy, "What do you think about checking into a motel so we could eat and freshen up before visiting the museum?"

Mommy thought it sounded like a great idea.

Daddy drove down the highway, away from all of the traffic. Finally, he pointed to a big, beautiful old home with a sign out front that said "Bed and Breakfast."

"I'll go in there and see if they have a room for us. No one, and I MEAN NO ONE, is to leave this car while I am gone!"

He didn't have to worry! No one even moved while he was gone. They all sat in silence waiting for his return.

Fortunately, Daddy was gone only a short while. Everyone was relieved when he came back. After the earlier events, they were all feeling a little afraid at the thought of being separated again. When he came back he had a big smile on his face and was holding a room key.

The rest of the Mouse family finally broke their silence when they saw Daddy smiling.

Mommy asked, "We're staying in THIS beautiful house? Can we afford it? It looks so expensive!"

Annie had never stayed overnight in a stranger's house. The house looked so big. She wondered if she would get lost in it! She was afraid to get out of the car.

"Annie, get out of the car," Daddy ordered. Annie shook her head, no. "I'm afraid," she sniffed.

Daddy put his arm around her. "Annie, we all make mistakes sometimes. You gave us all a pretty good scare, but the important thing is that you are safely back with us. I know you didn't mean to get lost."

Mommy looked at all of the children and said sternly, "Annie, you will be fine if you just remember to pay attention and stay with us. You all need to pay attention to each other a little bit better from now on. Now, get out of the car so we could check into our room and eat."

Annie got out of the car and walked beside Jenny. Her big sister always seemed to know the right thing to do. Maybe if she just stayed with Jenny everything would work out okay.

The whole family walked into the entryway of the home. Mommy gasped! She had never seen anything that looked so beautiful. She had been in the big house at the farm before, but it was nothing like this!

Daddy could tell she was pleased and said, "I promised you would get your special vacation. I wanted the first night away to be someplace really special. Wait till you see the room!"

They continued down the long hall and up the staircase to the second floor. Daddy stopped in front of the door with the number 3 on it and put the key in the door. They were all eagerly standing behind him, squealing, "Hurry up Daddy, we want to see the room!" Daddy teased them by opening the door very, very slowly. Even Mommy was getting excited.

"Wow!" they all shouted at once. This was much different than their home! It was beautiful; there was even wallpaper on the walls and carpeting with a flower pattern on the floor. The room was so big it even had a table for eating!

Annie, who had seen all of the signs announcing Illinois as the "Land of Lincoln" asked, "Do you suppose this is how the PRESIDENT lived?"

Everyone burst into laughter and Annie felt foolish for having said it. She really hated it when they all laughed at her! She decided to go find her own spot in the room. She was eager to curl up with her book and get away from the noise the others were making.

The rest of the mice children were running about the room, giggling and making a lot of noise.

"I'll take that spot, get away from me!"

"Stop pushing me!"

"Leave me alone."

Mommy broke in, "Everyone quiet down now! I will tell each of you where you will stay! But first, we are going to unpack, eat and freshen up. Sam and Bobby you two go back out to the car with Daddy and bring in the bags. Annie and Jenny, you two will help me in here. Annie? Annie? Where is Annie NOW?"

She looked around the room but didn't see Annie. She suddenly realized that she had not heard Annie's voice since everyone laughed at her.

"Did anyone see where Annie went," she asked.

They had not yet closed the door and wondered if Annie had wandered out of the room. Everyone knew how upset she got when people laughed at her. Did she run away?

Bobby asked, "Did she get lost-AGAIN?"

"I found her!" Daddy called. There, beside the couch by the fireplace, Annie was fast asleep.

"What a dope, scaring us all again," Jenny complained.

Startled, Annie jumped awake.

"Enough!" Mommy yelled. "Get those bags and let's eat!"

They all ran to do what was expected of them. Soon the table was set. There were crackers and three different kinds of cheese. What a feast! All but Annie came rushing to the table. They hadn't realized how hungry they had been. They couldn't wait to dig in.

"I don't deserve any of that food after I was such a bad girl today," Annie said as she began to sob.

Daddy ordered her to sit at the table with the rest of the family. "No one in this family will ever be punished by having food taken away! Get over here NOW!"

Annie didn't really feel that hungry after she had been so upset, but she knew when Daddy spoke like that to her she had better listen!

A short while later, with full bellies, and cameras in hand, they headed towards the Joliet Museum and Route 66 Visitor's Center. They crossed over a drawbridge right before getting to the museum. They had never been on one before.

Bobby said, "This is exciting! I always wanted to go over one of these!"

Once they parked the car and began walking to the Visitor's

Center, Annie decided to begin taking her pictures. She snapped a picture of the Visitor's Center and one of the drawbridge. She was starting to get back into the spirit of the trip!

Inside, a museum guide handed Mommy a map that showed all of the Route 66 attractions in Illinois.

Mommy said, "OH MY!" I thought it was just going to be a road to drive on! Look at all of this stuff we could see! It could take us a month just to drive through Illinois!"

Daddy warned that they would have to choose their stops carefully. "We'll never make it to the Grand Canyon if we stop to see everything!"

The guide showed them where they could sit to watch a video about Joliet and Illinois Route 66. Sam was so excited when he saw they were allowed to sit in the back ends of old cars to watch the video! The twins giggled as Daddy picked them up and placed them into one of the seats.

Daddy said it reminded him of the old Sky-Hi Drive-In Movie Theater that he and Mommy used to like to go to.

Sarah, Sandy and Sally all asked, "What's a drive-in"?

None of the Mouse children had ever been to a drive-in. Daddy said he would try to take them to one along the route if any were still open for business so they could experience it for themselves.

From the movie, the Mouse family learned Route 66 is sometimes called "The Mother Road" or "The Main Street of America." It goes through eight states and is more than 2000 miles long.

The children all exclaimed at once, "WOW, TWO THOUSAND MILES?!"

Annie asked Daddy if they would be going through ALL eight states and ALL 2000 miles. Daddy said they were going to try!

There was so much to do and see inside the Visitor's Center and Museum. After finishing their tour, Mommy went into the gift shop while the children had fun taking pictures inside the photo booth with Daddy.

When Mommy returned, she handed Sam a Route 66 Travel Guide for Kids. "I want you to share this with the other kids. You could take turns looking up places that might be fun for us to stop as we travel along the route."

Sam eagerly grabbed the book and began flipping through the pages to find Joliet. "Let's walk through town. It looks like there are some interesting places to see right here," he suggested.

Once outside, Daddy pointed out some of the historic buildings while the Mouse family walked all around the town. Annie wished they could have spent a day inside the big, beautiful library. How she wished her town had a library like that!

Mommy wished that there had been a special event in the beautiful, historic theater. She could only imagine how magnificent it would be.

When everyone started to complain that they couldn't walk another step, they decided it was time they headed back to the Bed & Breakfast. They were all exhausted, but happy. It wasn't long before all of the children were fast asleep.

Once the children were settled in for the night, Mommy and Daddy pulled out the map to discuss the stops for the next day. Mommy had relatives all over the country and wanted to visit Cousin Susie, who lived in Alton, Illinois, which was near St. Louis, Missouri. She wondered if they would be able to make it there by the following evening.

Daddy said, "That's clear across the state. If we're going to enjoy Route 66, we'd better count on spending two days before we make it to Alton. We'd better get some sleep; it will be a long day in the car tomorrow."

Chapter Eight:
Bed & Breakfast Fit for a Royal Family

The next morning the delicious smells coming from downstairs woke the Mouse family up. Boy did it smell good! Since Annie didn't have much of an appetite the day before, she was really hungry now! She wondered what they would be having for breakfast. She didn't think there were any leftovers from last night.

Daddy told them all to get ready. "Help your mother with the little ones," he instructed. "When everyone is ready, we will go downstairs and get our breakfast."

"You mean we get to have that food that smells so good?" Annie squealed!

"What did you think a Bed & Breakfast was?" Jenny asked, as she rolled her eyes.

Annie said she had no idea since she had never been to one before. "Quit trying to make me feel dumb, Jenny," Annie pouted.

While Mommy repacked their bags, Annie, Jenny, Sam and Bobby each helped one of the little ones get dressed. They were eager to have breakfast!

Finally, they reached the room where all of the good smells were coming from. They could not believe their eyes when they walked into the dining room! They had never seen so much food at once.

There was a big table set with pretty dishes. Their hostess greeted them. "Good morning! I hope you're hungry! Take a plate and help yourselves. Let me know if there is anything else you need."

Mommy reminded them all to remember their manners. "Your eyes are bigger than your stomachs. Only take as much as you could eat," she directed.

Annie's eyes got very big when she saw the basket of strawberries! She LOVED strawberries!

Mommy suggested that Annie have toast with her strawberries. "Too many strawberries might give you a tummy ache."

Annie didn't want that to happen. She took a slice, then noticed the basket of all different flavors of jelly. She had a hard time deciding which to choose since they all looked so good. Their hostess said they were all made in her kitchen.

They all took a place at the table. Mommy said she felt like a queen at this huge table. Annie asked if that made Daddy a king and the rest of the family princes and princesses. She knew she felt like a princess in this beautiful room with all this food!

Mommy said, "Daddy, I don't know how you found this place, but I love it!" Daddy grinned at the compliment. He liked pleasing his family.

There was another family already seated at the table. After introductions, they discovered the other family was from Canada and on a Route 66 trip, too. The little girl, Mary, was the same age as Annie and throughout breakfast they shared stories about their schools and friends. Annie was surprised to learn that the school in Canada seemed just like her school. They were even learning the same things!

After everyone had eaten and they thanked their hostess, Daddy teased, "Well, I guess we could start for home now. We don't need to go to the Grand Canyon after having this meal fit for a Royal Family!"

"No, Daddy!" they all squealed together. "We still want to see the Grand Canyon!!"

"Well, we'd better say good-bye to our new friends and get back on the road then. Let's pack up the car and get on our way!"

"Everyone, use the bathroom before getting back in the car," Mommy reminded. "While I'm waiting for everyone to finish up I'll call Susie and let her know we are on our way to her house."

Chapter Nine:
Illinois: The Land of Lincoln... and so Much More!

Back in the car, Mommy said that she had the best homemade breakfast that she had ever eaten- that SHE didn't have to cook herself.

Daddy said he enjoyed staying in a big house that he didn't have to do all the work in! They both looked happy.

As Daddy began driving down the road, Mommy said, "Kids, we're going to have another long day ahead of us. Why don't you take out your notebooks and record the names of the towns we pass through? You could also look through the guidebook for fun stops along the way."

Traveling through Wilmington, Bobby suddenly yelled, "Stop the car, Daddy! Look at that spaceman!"

Daddy slammed on the brakes and they all turned to look in the direction Bobby was pointing. They saw the largest statue they'd ever seen of a big green spaceman!

Bobby quickly referred to the guidebook and told everyone, "The Gemini Giant is one of several statues known as "Muffler Men" because at one time statues like these were used to advertise automobile mufflers and tires." This one now stood outside a diner that didn't appear to be open.

They all got out of the car to take pictures in front of The Gemini Giant. Annie knew she wanted to put this one in her scrapbook!

As soon as Annie finished taking her picture, she was eager to continue their journey. She ran to the car, yelling "Come on everyone! Don't you want to see what else we could find?"

Daddy was happy to see that Annie was back to her old self and excited about the trip again.

It wasn't long before they were in Braidwood. This time it was Mommy who pointed out some statues alongside the Polk-a-Dot Drive-In Diner.

Daddy stopped the car so he and Mommy could take a closer look at them. Mommy and Daddy seemed excited to see these statues of movie stars, but none of the children recognized any of them!

Daddy pulled into a parking spot. "This looks like a good place to have lunch! I want to see what's inside."

Daddy was excited looking at all of the neat stuff inside while waiting for their hamburgers to be ready.

Annie pointed to a tall, colorful box and asked, "What's that?"

Daddy said it played records and was called a "juke box."

Annie and her brothers and sisters weren't sure they knew what records were, so Daddy said he'd show them. He put some coins in the box and pushed a button. They all watched as a small round disk came forward; suddenly they could hear Elvis Presley singing, "Jail House Rock!"

Annie decided that was her favorite thing in the diner! Daddy said his favorite was the statue of Elvis Presley. Just then, their burgers were ready and the Mouse family sat down for lunch.

After they finished eating Daddy said he thought his tummy would burst, he was so stuffed! Everyone agreed and Mommy said they would have to waddle back to the car!

In Gardner, Daddy pulled the car into the parking lot of The Riviera Restaurant. "This was the restaurant where Al Capone used to hang out," he said. "Our travel guide said it was something to see. Too bad it's not open right now."

Annie asked who Al Capone was and Sam said she'd learn about him when she got older. Annie sighed. She was tired of hearing, "when you get older" when she asked questions!

They also discovered an old horse-drawn streetcar sitting behind the restaurant. Annie wanted to take some pictures. Daddy told her to hurry since there was so much more to see in Illinois!

They got out of the car again to explore in downtown Gardner.

A man was unlocking a tiny building and told the Mouse family to go inside. Annie followed her brothers inside, but quickly ran out! It turned out to be a jail! She thought it was really cool to see, but didn't think it would be much fun to be in there for too long!

The man told them everyone in town was excited that the street car behind The Riviera Restaurant was going to be moved near the jail and turned into a diner. "It will take a while to restore it, but it will be great when it's done," he added.

As they walked back to the car, Sam asked if their next stop could be in Dwight. He had been reading the guidebook and was excited to learn that there was a bank building designed by Frank Lloyd Wright in that town[1]. Sam said he'd read about Frank Lloyd Wright in his Social Studies book and hoped that someday they would have a chance to see his most famous building of all-- Fallingwater, which was only a few hours from where they lived. Bobby thought it would be exciting to see a building by the famous architect. He said, "Next year when I'm in Social Studies I could tell everyone in my class that I got to see a Frank Lloyd Wright building!"

It was settled; Dwight would be their next stop.

Once in Dwight, Mommy said, "What a cute little town. I think I could spend all day here!" Daddy said he wondered if they'd EVER make it to California!

They decided to drive through the town and only look at the bank building. Sam was pleased to see that he recognized some of the "classic Frank Lloyd Wright features" that he learned about in his Social Studies book. Annie had NO idea WHAT he was talking about, but she liked the ceiling in the bank building!

A few miles down the road, Daddy stopped again in Odell at what looked like an old gas station but was now another Visitor's Center. Daddy wanted to see the inside of the building so they all got out again. Inside, Mommy bought some post cards of the building. Annie was glad because she didn't think she could get the whole building in one of her photographs. A guide inside the center told them that they just HAD to stop in Pontiac and see the museum there, along with some really great murals around the town.

1   Scan the code for more information on the Frank Lloyd Wright Bank
Building or visit http://tinyurl.com/m9kdwhb.

The triplets, Sandy, Sarah, and Sally all asked in unison, "What's a mural?"

Daddy said when they got to Pontiac and found one, they would understand.

Holding the guidebook, Jenny teased, "I'm looking at a picture of one now!"

Sally cried, "That's not FAIR! We can't see it!"

"KIDS!" Daddy warned sternly.

They instantly got quiet. They ALL knew what that tone meant! Bobby suggested they start playing the license plate game again.

A short while later, Daddy pointed to a sign that said, "ROAD ENDS."

"What are we supposed to do now?" Annie wondered.

Jenny read from the guidebook that parts of Route 66 were destroyed, so it was no longer possible to do the entire route without getting on the interstate for awhile.

As Daddy steered the car towards the freeway entrance ramp, he reassured them he'd been expecting this to happen. As he turned the radio on, Daddy said, "Let's listen to some music for awhile since there's not much to see right now."

Midway through the first song, Mommy said, "Daddy, turn the radio up. There's breaking news."

They all gasped when they heard the announcer say, "Firefighters are in Gardner. The Riviera Restaurant is engulfed in flames. Initial reports indicate the building is a total loss."[2]

Annie screeched, "We were just there! I can't believe it's on fire!"

Mommy replied, "I'm glad we had a chance to see it before the fire."

As they entered Pontiac, they came upon a huge painting on

---

2   The Riviera burned to the ground on June 8, 2010. The streetcar was moved to the center of town near the Gardner jail.

the side of a building. It had the Route 66 shield and the words PONTIAC, ILLINOIS on it. Daddy pointed to it and said, "Kids, THAT'S a mural!" Annie was eager to get out her camera again!

Daddy wanted to see the museum, but Mommy wanted to take a walk around the town to see more murals, so they decided to split up for a little bit. "Let's meet back here in 90 minutes," Mommy suggested.

Annie and her big brothers and sister went with Daddy, while Mommy walked around town with the little ones. Annie knew she'd have a chance to see the rest of the murals once they were back in the car anyway.

Daddy loved looking at all of the old things that reminded him of HIS childhood and Annie liked to hear Daddy's explanations. As they were leaving the museum, the guide told them not to miss the stop for maple syrup in Shirley. Daddy liked how everyone was so friendly and helpful!

When they came out of the museum, Mommy was walking towards them on the sidewalk. Daddy said, "Perfect timing! Are you ready to continue our adventure?"

Mommy asked, "Can we stop in Shirley at a syrup place? Everyone I talked to said it's a stop we shouldn't miss!"

Daddy laughed and said that's what he was about to tell HER!

Daddy said they would have to hurry if they were going to make it to the syrup place before it closed. Jenny didn't know what all the fuss was about syrup! Couldn't you get syrup anywhere?

They all enjoyed the ride on Route 66 to Funk's Grove. It was lined with trees and reminded them of the area where they lived. When they finally pulled into the drive, they discovered that the store would be closing in five minutes. Mommy told Daddy to stay in the car with the kids while she went inside.

When she came back, Mommy said she had a special treat for them as she handed each of the children a maple candy leaf. Annie didn't want to eat it at first since it looked so pretty, but boy was it good! Jenny had to admit that she didn't expect to get candy from a syrup place! Mommy said she also bought a few bottles of syrup that were shaped like leaves and a jug that said, "Pure Maple Sirup" on the label[3].

They nibbled on their candy until their next stop, which was in Atlanta. Annie was so excited when they saw another Muffler Man! This one was holding a giant hot dog! They ALL giggled at the sight. Daddy parked the car so Annie could take pictures. That's when Annie saw the library building with a really cool shape. Annie wanted to go inside, but was disappointed to find that it was already closed for the day.

Daddy drove through Springfield without stopping or even slowing down enough for Annie to be able to take any pictures. Route 66 was busy with traffic and the one way streets were confusing to Daddy. Daddy said it was just his luck to be driving through during "rush hour!"

Sam was reading his guidebook and said that it was too late to see Lincoln's house and tomb anyway.

It seemed everyone was noticing something they wanted Daddy to stop for.

Mommy noticed the Cozy Dog Drive In just as Daddy was passing it.

Bobby shouted, "Look, there's another Muffler Man!"

Annie tried to take a picture through the car window, but it just looked like a blur! Annie cried, "Daaa-deee, PLEASE slow down, I want to take some pictures!"

Daddy sounded angry when he said he was sorry that he couldn't just slam on the brakes in traffic just so she could take pictures! Annie was happy she got to see the Muffler Man, and knew she'd better not say anything else to Daddy.

Mommy said, "Daddy, don't you remember we agreed to stop at the Cozy Dog Drive-In and get one of the famous hot dogs on a stick?"

"Yes, I DID want to stop there," Daddy agreed. "I think I remember passing it by. I'll find someplace to turn around and go back. Everyone, look for the sign so that I could stop in enough time to turn," Daddy ordered.

---

3   Scan the code for more information on Funks Grove Maple Sirup or
     visit http://tinyurl.com/lojqluf.

COZY DOG DRIVE IN
SPRINGFIELD, ILLINOIS

Moments later, everyone saw the two hot dogs hugging, high on top of the sign and shouted excitedly, "Slow down, Daddy! There it is!"

"I see it," Daddy responded as he slowed the car down and turned into the parking lot.

Inside, Mommy stood at the counter to place their order while Daddy was supposed to choose a place to sit with the children. But Daddy kept stopping to admire the artwork of the famous Route 66 artist, Bob Waldmire, that was displayed on the walls.

"I read in our guidebook that the Cozy Dog Drive-In is owned by the Waldmire family. That's why I couldn't pass this place up," Daddy explained.

Mommy motioned to Daddy to help her carry the food trays.

"We'll look at the artwork after we finish eating," Daddy said as he settled the children at a table.

Sam wanted to learn more and quickly gobbled his corn dog and began reading from his guidebook again. "Did you know that Ed Waldmire, Jr.- he was Bob's father- created the cozy dog? He first called it a 'crusty cur' but his wife didn't like that name," Sam rambled.

Everyone laughed and Mommy said, "I agree with his wife. Would we be sitting here eating 'crusty curs'"?

Annie said she liked her cozy dog. "A cozy dog sounds yummy and it IS! A crusty cur doesn't sound like something I'd want to eat!"

"Well, if I ever invent a food item, I'll be sure to have Mommy name it," Daddy joked. "Let's finish up so we can look at all this great Route 66 artwork."

"We could spend all day looking at it. I can't believe anyone could draw such detail so tiny! This is amazing," Mommy exclaimed.

Annie tugged on Daddy's arm. "Daddy, could you pick me up? I can't see!"

He hoisted Annie up on his shoulders. "Wow!" she exclaimed!

And of course, all of the younger children wanted their turn on Daddy's shoulders, too. With the last one satisfied he'd seen enough, Daddy said it was time to leave.

As they made their way back to the car, Daddy was the first to admit that he was glad he turned around and came back to the Cozy Dog Drive-In. Not only was the food great, they also got to see some of Bob Waldmire's artwork[4].

Mommy suggested getting a room for the night in Springfield, so they could see some of the Lincoln historic sites in the morning.

"Maybe on the way back home we could stop in Springfield again. There's still so much so see and do here," Daddy said. "But for now, I just want to get out of traffic and continue our Route 66 adventure."

Daddy didn't stop again until he reached Mount Olive. Sam read from the guidebook that there were a few historic places that they should be sure to stop and see: the Soulsby Shell Station and the Mother Jones Monument.

Mommy told Daddy to stop the car in the shopping district so she could ask in one of the shops where those places could be found. It took Mommy a LONG time to come back to the car and when she did, she was carrying several bags. Mommy said the people in the shop were so friendly and nice; she just had to buy some souvenirs from them! Daddy rolled his eyes and laughed and asked if she remembered to get the directions.

Mommy told Daddy that the Mother Jones Monument was actually a grave marker in a cemetery just a short distance away. Jenny groaned and Annie said it was okay with her if they decided not to stop. Daddy laughed and said he'd like to see it. Bobby and Sam agreed that they'd like to stop, too. Daddy said that they could stay in the car while he and the boys took a quick look. On the drive

---

4   Bob Waldmire died on December 16, 2009. His artwork lives on all across Route 66. A very special thank you to the Waldmire family, especially his brother Buz, for providing information and Bob's illustrations for inclusion in this book. Scan the code for more information about Bob and to purchase his artwork http://www.bobwaldmire.com.

38

to the cemetery, Sam continued to read from the guidebook and learned that the monument was erected to honor the woman who supported the miners in a labor dispute a long time ago. Annie didn't understand what a labor dispute was, but Sam told her she would learn all about it in Social Studies when she got older[5].

After driving through the cemetery and taking some pictures, Daddy continued on to the gas station. It was Mommy's turn to stay in the car with the little ones; she was more interested in the shops, but Daddy loved looking at anything that had to do with gas stations and old signs. There was something for everyone to enjoy in Mount Olive!

Jenny had pestered Sam to give her a turn with the guidebook when he got out of the car with Daddy. She was really getting interested in reading it and wasn't ready to give it back to Sam when he came back to the car.

Suddenly, Jenny got excited and shouted, "I know where we have to stop next! Henry's Rabbit Ranch in Staunton! It looks cool!"

Daddy asked where it was and Jenny said the map showed that it wasn't too far from Mount Olive, so it shouldn't be far.

Sam pulled the guidebook from Jenny and said, "Let me see, you don't even know how to read a map!"

"Sam," Daddy said sternly.

The way Daddy said his name, Sam knew it was a warning! He quickly handed the book back to Jenny and muttered, "Sorry, Jenny."

Suddenly the triplets were giggling and pointing at a statue of a huge rabbit beside the old gas station.

Mommy said, "I guess we found Henry's Rabbit Ranch!"

Daddy pulled into the driveway and everyone got out quickly. All the kids raced to get to the huge bunny statue, giggling as they ran. Mommy told them not to fight over it; they'd all have a chance to sit on it. Annie wanted a picture with Daddy standing beside it for her scrap book so Bobby snapped it for her.

Mr. Henry came out and introduced himself. Daddy seemed excited as he asked about all the old cars and trucks parked outside.

Annie was getting bored with all of the talk of old cars. She

---

5   Scan the code for more information about Mother Jones or visit http://tinyurl.com/l3be2jm.

wanted to know if there were any REAL rabbits around.

Mr. Henry replied, "A few, but we'll have to go inside to see them!"

When they stepped inside, the Mouse children were excited to see all of the rabbits! They even got to pet one named Big Red[6]! Big Red even "autographed" a post card for them by nibbling on it! Before the kids had a chance to fight over it, Mommy said SHE'D keep it and put it in a special scrap book that they'd make of the trip when they got home.

Mommy told Mr. Henry how disappointed they all were that Daddy wouldn't stop in Springfield so they could see Lincoln's home and the historic district.

Mr. Henry told them they could see another Lincoln historic site that wouldn't take them through too much traffic or too far off of Route 66.

"You will have to back-track a bit to get to Vandalia," he said while showing Daddy how to get there on a map. "And you will have to take the interstate to get back to Route 66 when you're done in Vandalia. And there's no avoiding the St. Louis traffic as you continue west," he warned.

Everyone enjoyed meeting Mr. Henry and felt like they'd made a new friend. After they said good-bye to him all of the Mouse children started to talk at once, "Can we go there, huh, Daddy? Can we? Can we, PLEEEEASE?!"

Daddy said it was up to Mommy. Mommy said she only wanted to go out of the way to see Vandalia if they would still be able to stop and see Cousin Susie in Alton. Daddy said the trip was for her, so if she wanted to do both, it was fine by him.

It was settled! They were on their way to Vandalia.

---

6   Even though Big Red went to Animal Heaven in December, 2012, there are still many special bunnies to visit at Henry's Rabbit Ranch.

Chapter Ten:
An Unexpected Side Trip

Mr. Henry was right; it really wasn't that far off of their route. Before too long, Daddy pulled up to a big white building and announced, "Well, here we are in Vandalia, in front of what was once the capitol building of Illinois."

They walked into the building and learned that this building was the county's courthouse before it was the Capitol Building. They saw where Lincoln sat as a state legislator before he was the President of the country.

Annie couldn't believe that they were standing in the same place that President Lincoln once stood. She knew he was important because they made an "Abe Lincoln" bulletin board to celebrate President's Day at her school. She remembered learning that no matter how poor you might be as a child, you could still grow up to be the president of the United States!

As they went through the building they were able to see how life was for people in the 1800s. There was a wood stove that heated the rooms, candles that provided the lighting and the original tables where Lincoln once sat.

They also saw the inkwells and feathers, that Daddy called quills, that were used for writing. The wooden floors reminded Annie of her home. This was one of the tallest buildings Annie had ever been in and she felt very small standing in it.

The Mouse family didn't stay inside very long. They took a walk around the outside of the building and stopped at a huge statue of a woman who was holding a baby and had another child hanging on to her leg.

Daddy read the words on the base and told them that it said, "Madonna of the Trail" and explained that it was a memorial for the pioneer mothers during the covered wagon days.

The Mouse family walked around the block and found a diner to have lunch. While waiting for their food they talked about how beautiful the building was and how interesting it was to see what life was like back in the 1800s. They talked about the woman on the statue. She didn't look happy. They wondered about how hard life must have been while traveling across the country in a covered wagon. They were all very quiet as they thought about the mother who looked very sad.

Bobby said he had read that a lot of people died as they traveled across the country in the covered wagons. He said what they had all been thinking: "I guess lots of babies died, too. I never really thought about it before, but it makes me feel sad."

They continued to eat their lunch in silence as they thought about everything they just saw. Annie said, "I guess we are pretty lucky today. Everything is so much easier than it used to be. I guess Lincoln was one of those people who helped make life better for everyone, huh?"

Mommy said, "I'm glad we don't have to travel in covered wagons today! It's nice that we are having an adventure when transportation is so much easier!"

Chapter Eleven:
Daddy's Turn to Get Lost

Back in the car, the Mouse children decided to start the license plate game again. It seemed to Mommy that they were all talking at once. They were starting to get louder and louder.

"I just saw a Florida license plate!"

"I saw it first!"

"Too bad. I CALLED it first!"

"No fair."

"You're squishing me. MOVE OVER!"

"You move over."

"MAWWWW-MY!"

Daddy hollered, "Enough!"

When Daddy raised his voice, they KNEW he meant business! They all quieted down. Daddy suggested they each get out their notebooks and pencils and make a list of the cars and license plates, then compare notes in fifteen minutes.

By the time they reached the signs directing them to St. Louis there was so much traffic that the children had a hard time keeping up with all the license plates!

Daddy wasn't used to driving in this kind of traffic. He thought Springfield was bad, but this was much worse! He was starting to get grumpy. Mommy was telling him which lanes to get into and helping direct his driving. This "help" just seemed to irritate him.

"Daddy, I think you are going the wrong way. Why don't you stop and ask for directions?" Mommy suggested.

Daddy sighed and said loudly, "I know where I am going! I don't need to stop and ask for directions."

Mommy said, "But Cousin Susie lives in Alton and that's north of the interstate, before getting to St. Louis. The sign we just passed said we are going south on the interstate and it looks like we are headed to East St. Louis. WE ARE GOING THE WRONG WAY!!"

Daddy decided to get off at the next exit to get gas. Suddenly, Annie called from the back, "Hey, what's that huge catsup bottle up in the sky?" They all looked up and, sure enough, it WAS the biggest catsup bottle they had ever seen! It was very curious indeed.

Daddy got out of the car to pump the gas. He asked the gas station attendant where they were and was told they were in Collinsville and the big catsup bottle was actually the town's water tower. Mommy nudged Daddy and pointed to Collinsville and Alton on the map she was holding. Daddy had to admit it; she was right, he had gone the wrong way. They would have to get back on the interstate and go in the opposite direction, where it looked like they would be stuck in traffic.

No one but Annie was in a good mood after that! She was excited about the great photograph she'd been able to take of the catsup bottle so she was glad they'd gotten lost. She didn't think it was a good time to mention it, though. Annie and her brothers and sisters decided it was a good time for another nap. Secretly, Annie was afraid Daddy would be too irritated to want to continue to the Grand Canyon if anyone fussed now.

Chapter Twelve:
A Visit with Cousin Susie

It was late by the time they got to Cousin Susie's house. Once Daddy turned off the highway, they had no problem finding the right road. They all breathed a sigh of relief. Cousin Susie told them to look for the first dirt road to the right. Susie and her family lived in the only house on the road.

Susie heard the station wagon on the road and came outside to greet her company. Mommy saw Susie waving to them long before the car pulled up to the shed.

Susie came running up to the station wagon and threw her arms around Mommy as soon as she got out of the car. "SUSIE!" Mommy shouted. "How much I've missed you!"

Susie hugged each of the children and squealed, "Look at you! All grown up!" She pinched Annie's cheeks and Annie hugged her tight. It was great to see Cousin Susie, even if Annie hated having her cheeks pinched!

Susie said, "You must be starved by now! How come you're so late?"

Everyone looked at Daddy. Mommy just glared at Daddy and said, "SOMEONE wouldn't stop and ask for directions."

Even though she had been upset with Daddy for being so stubborn, Annie now felt bad for him when she saw his shoulders slump. He looked ashamed when he said, "The traffic was bad near St. Louis and I went the wrong way. I guess I got confused."

Susie laughed and said, "Well, it looks like you are having a typical family vacation! It's not a real family vacation unless you get lost at least once and everyone gets irritated with everyone else! So, it sounds like you are having the perfect vacation! Come on in and let's have dinner!"

Mommy and Daddy looked at each other and started to laugh. They were here with family, why stay angry?

Mommy said, "You know, we wouldn't have seen that huge catsup bottle if we hadn't gotten lost. That really WAS something to see, wasn't it, kids?" All the children started to giggle and everyone agreed they enjoyed the side trip.

With everyone in better spirits, they followed Susie into the dining room. The table was set and they were eager to eat!

Mommy said, "Susie, how you fussed! We didn't want you to go through any trouble for us!"

In no time at all everyone was eating, talking and laughing all at the same time. Cousin Susie always made Mommy smile. Annie liked seeing Mommy so happy.

The whole Mouse family slept on the living room floor that night. Annie pretended they were camping out. Since they'd had a long, exciting day, everyone fell asleep quickly.

When Mommy and Daddy woke up they could smell the coffee already brewing. Cousin Susie was putting out her prettiest mugs. Mommy started to protest but Susie insisted that she liked having a reason to use her "company" mugs.

Daddy said, "Susie, I wanted to treat you to breakfast! I hope you haven't started to make anything."

Susie squealed with delight. "It's been a long time since I went out to eat! That sounds like fun!"

Daddy joked, "Just tell me where you'd like to go. AND tell me how to get there!"

Mommy just looked at him and decided against saying anything about getting lost the previous night.

"I know! Instead of going out to breakfast, I'll make it here and then ride with you to St. Louis. We'll get a special treat there. I don't get to St. Louis often, but love to shop there. I'll take the bus back home."

Mommy thought this was a great idea, since they would have even more time to spend together. "But what's the special treat you have in mind?" Mommy asked.

"Ted Drewes Frozen Custard is a favorite Route 66 stop," Susie answered. "If you're going through St. Louis, and exploring Route 66, it's a treat you shouldn't miss[7]."

"Frozen custard? What's THAT?" Sarah, Sandy, and Sally all asked at once.

"It's like ice cream- the best ice cream you've ever eaten!" Susie answered. She reassured them that they would not be disappointed! She thought a light breakfast of toast and fruit would be all that they would need if they were going for frozen custard.

Everyone hurried into the kitchen to help with breakfast. They were excited thinking about getting another special treat. The children rushed through breakfast and ran to the car, pushing each other and shouting, "Let me in first, I'm the oldest, I get to choose first, move over!"

Daddy yelled, "STOP! Freeze! Cousin Susie is getting in the car first and you will all mind your manners!"

Daddy explained that Cousin Susie would get the front seat, next to Mommy since she would be giving Daddy driving directions. Daddy did NOT want to get lost in traffic again!

With everyone settled, Susie directed them back onto the highway. "Everyone sit back and relax; it'll take a little while to get there," Susie said.

As Daddy drove slowly through the traffic, Susie asked if they would like to see the Old Chain of Rocks Bridge. Susie explained that they could see it from Illinois or Missouri since it connects the two states and goes over the Mississippi River. "It's really interesting to see, since it has a bend in the middle of it. It's no longer used for vehicles, but you could walk over it," she added.

They decided to make Chain of Rocks Bridge their last stop in Illinois. It began to rain as Daddy was parking the car. Just as they were about to get out of the car, a police officer drove up and told

---

7   Scan the code to learn more about Ted Drewes or visit http://tinyurl.com/87gr68o.

everyone they had to leave because the area was being closed due to a flash flood warning!

Annie quickly took a picture of the bridge from inside the car. Suddenly, the sky got very black and it began raining so hard that it was difficult to see the road in front of them. Annie could tell Daddy was worried and she began to cry. Daddy told Annie not to worry as he followed the other cars out of the area.

Once they were away from the river the rain stopped as suddenly as it had begun. Daddy looked relieved. Everyone was shocked to see how quickly the weather could turn!

As they drove towards the Gateway Arch, Susie asked the children, "Did you know that you are about to see the tallest national monument in the United States?" She also told them that a ride takes people all the way to the top of the arch.

Mommy asked Daddy if he wanted to ride up into the arch. Before he could answer, Annie shouted, "Look ahead! I can see IT!"

They all started to squeal with excitement. What a sight! It looked so big! Daddy and Mommy looked at each other.

Daddy was the first to talk, "Mommy, do you REALLY want to go up that high?"

Annie was always afraid of heights. She interrupted, "No, Daddy, I don't wanna go up there."

Sam was relieved that Annie said it first; he didn't want to be the one that sounded like a coward, but it looked pretty scary to him, too.

Susie finally spoke, "I've never been on the ride myself, but I'm not sure I'd want to go up in this kind of weather. You can always stop on the way back home if you decide you want to do it."

Mommy said she thought that was a good idea. Everyone looked relieved. Secretly, none of them really wanted to take the ride because they were ALL afraid of heights.

Bobby was the first to ask when they were getting their frozen custard. Susie directed them through the traffic and soon they were in the parking lot of the popular Route 66 landmark. Several people were lined up waiting to place their orders. Mommy said she'd order first with the twins since they were starting to get fussy.

Annie was thankful that she would have to wait a little while. It always took her a long time to decide when there were so many choices! She didn't think they would ever be here again, and she didn't want to make the wrong choice. When it was her turn to order, she said the first thing that came to mind: chocolate! Annie loved chocolate so she thought it was the best choice and BOY was it good!

Jenny pointed to the twins and said, "EWW! What's wrong with them? Why are they such slobs?"

Sam said, "How do you think YOU looked when you were eating ice cream when you were THAT little, Jenny?"

Jenny was about to answer Sam when she caught Daddy's eye. She turned away without saying anything more.

After one look at the twins' faces, Daddy thought it would be a good idea to finish their treats before getting back in the car.

Mommy said it was a good thing she'd packed the wipes, since it looked like they were wearing as much as they were eating! She added, "Thanks for showing us this place, Susie! I think everyone enjoyed their treats!"

All the kids nodded in agreement and rushed to give Susie a hug. Susie giggled and said that she was glad the twins had already been cleaned up!

With their treats finished, it was time to drop Susie off and get back on the road. Susie directed Daddy through traffic to the area where she wanted to shop. He parked the car by the curb and they all got out to give her one last hug to say good-bye.

Before Daddy pulled away, Susie made sure he knew the right way to go. Even Daddy laughed this time. Susie always did know how to make everyone laugh. They would miss her.

Annie kept waving until Susie was out of sight.

Chapter Thirteen:
Route 66 Adventures through Missouri

As the car rolled away, the children continued to talk about the visit with Cousin Susie. She was so much fun; they wished she lived closer so they could visit with her more often.

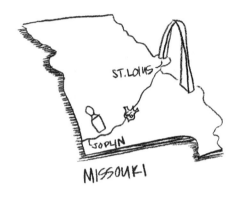

"I need you kids to be really quiet now. I'm going to be driving in heavy traffic again and need to concentrate on driving," Daddy said.

Mommy handed each child another piece of the maple leaf candy. "Why don't you get out your notebooks and continue to write down the names of the towns we drive through," she suggested to the older children.

Annie wished they had thought about doing that as soon as they left home. She wanted to tell her best friend, Molly Mole, all the places she had been and she knew she would never remember all of the names by the time they got home.

Annie had barely finished writing "St. Louis" in her notebook, when Daddy stopped the car again. Daddy said his nerves were a little frazzled from driving through the St. Louis traffic and he needed a break!

They all got out to explore the Route 66 State Park Visitor's Center Museum and Gift Shop. Daddy and Mommy enjoyed reading about the history of Missouri Route 66 and looking at old newspaper clippings.

The twins were starting to get fussy; they weren't too interested in the old newspaper stories, so Mommy asked at the desk what stops they could make along the way that the little ones would enjoy.

The clerk replied, "You'll ALL enjoy both the Meramec Caverns and the Jesse James Museum in Stanton."

Big Brothers Sam and Bobby got excited because they knew who Jesse James was! Bobby shouted, "Daddy, could we go to the caverns and The Jesse James Museum?" They couldn't wait to learn more about the famous outlaw!

Mommy took over driving so Daddy could relax on the way to the caverns. She didn't mind driving the less crowded Route 66.

The boys talked excitedly about Jesse James and pretended to shoot each other while the car thumped along through Pacific and Saint Clair before they finally arrived at The Meramec Caverns in Stanton.

A marker at the entrance said that the caverns were used by Jesse James as a hideout. Bobby and Sam were so excited they started to run ahead of the rest of the family. Mommy had to remind everyone to slow down and stay together.

Annie made sure to stay very close to Daddy as they walked into the cave. She did NOT want to get lost again.

When Daddy paid the admission the lady said, "You're in luck! The next tour starts in five minutes!"

The tour was really interesting! Annie discovered that Sam and Bobby hadn't lied to her when they told her that Jesse James was a train and bank robber. Annie never could tell when they were having fun with her or when something was true!

The tour guide said that Jesse James and his gang really did hide out in the caverns[8]. He also told them about saltpeter, used to make gunpowder, being mined there long ago.

Annie and Jenny thought the stalactites and stalagmites were really cool! The whole family enjoyed the light show in the theatre room at the end of the tour. Even Jenny had to admit that she had a good time!

When the tour was over, they went into the huge gift shop. Daddy told them they each could pick out ONE special souvenir. Once they spent their money, Daddy warned, they couldn't buy anything else for the rest of the trip so they should choose wisely!

Mommy added, "We'll be making lots of stops, so make sure

---

8   Scan the code for more information on Meramec Caverns or visit http://tinyurl.com/mtlxoxs.

whatever you pick out will be special enough that you won't ask for anything else!"

Annie always did have trouble making choices. She didn't want to make a mistake and get something only to find she wanted something else in a day or two. This was going to be so hard for her! Mommy reminded her they'd be coming back this way on the way home, so if there was something she thought she wanted, but wasn't sure, she could always wait and get it on the way home. THAT made Annie feel better!

Sam picked up a rubber snake and swung it around at the other children before Daddy stopped him. Daddy warned, "If you keep teasing the little ones, I won't let you get anything at all." Sam put it down and quickly apologized.

Bobby asked if they could go to the Jesse James museum next. Mommy said that it would probably be closed by the time they got there if they didn't leave right away. They all agreed they'd rather see the museum than look for souvenirs.

Back outside, they were all shocked to discover how hot it was compared to inside the caverns! Now they understood why the tour guide said that people used to come to the caves to keep cool in the hot summer months!

The Jesse James Museum was only a few miles away so they were there in a few minutes. Mommy, Daddy, Sam and Bobby seemed to know a lot about Jesse James and were very excited about going through the museum.

Inside, Annie saw all kinds of old tools that were used in the 1800s, but she had NO idea what they were! Mommy and Daddy explained that many of the things aren't needed anymore because of modern technology. Daddy explained that before electricity, there were no power tools and everything had to be done by hand.

They also learned that Jesse James might really have lived to be an old man! Sam wondered why his Social Studies textbook said that Jesse James died while being captured. The museum guide pointed to a "Wanted Dead or Alive" poster on the wall and explained that Jesse James might have faked his death so people would stop looking for him.

Once they were settled back in the car, Sam said, "I bet they made up all that stuff about Jesse James being alive until he was over 100 years old! My textbook wouldn't have wrong information in it, would it?"

Daddy explained that sometimes things are believed to be true for a long time, but then as time goes by more information is learned or better technology provides ways to examine things more carefully.

Bobby asked, "Like when they used to believe that the earth was flat?" and Daddy replied, "Exactly!"

Sam said he couldn't wait to go back to school in the fall and tell his teachers all about what he learned!

Annie grabbed her notebook so she could write down the towns of Stanton, Sullivan, St. Cloud and Bourbon as they drove along.

Daddy pointed to the water tower with the town's name of "Bourbon" written on it and wondered if it was really filled with water. Sam and Bobby laughed, but Annie didn't understand why.

She asked, "Daddy, what's so funny?"

Daddy said, "Never mind, you'll understand when you're older."

Annie hated whenever she got that answer! She wanted to know NOW, NOT when she was older. She felt like they were making fun of her for being little.

Before she could pout about it, her sister interrupted. Jenny had been reading the guidebook and said that they would soon be in Cuba, the "Route 66 Mural City."

"Can we stop there?" Annie asked.

Daddy said he thought they could drive right through Cuba and see the murals from the car, but if there were special ones they really wanted to see, he would stop.

As soon as they got into town, they could tell why it was called the Route 66 Mural City! There were amazing murals all over the town; the scenes on the sides of the buildings looked so real!

Daddy soon realized he'd have to park the car so they could walk up and down the street to really enjoy the murals.

Bobby said he'd like to be able to paint like that one day. Annie took lots of pictures all over town. She said it was going to be really hard to choose which photos to print out and put into her photo journal!

Mommy said she had seen a sign for the World's Largest Rocking Chair while they were driving towards Cuba and wondered where it was. "I'll just go in one of the shops and ask," she said.

When she came out she had a bag of chocolate fudge for the family to share. Annie was glad she chose a candy store to go into!

Mommy told Daddy that the Rocking Chair was only a few miles down the road at the Fanning US 66 Outpost and General Store. Everyone was eager to see it.

Bobby said to the other kids, "I'll race you back to the car" and off they ran down the street with Bobby in the lead.

On the corner Annie started to say, "Excuse me" as they ran past a group of people before she realized they weren't people at all; they were part of the mural painted on the side of the building! As they piled back into the car, Daddy said, "When you think the people in a painting are real, you KNOW it's good artwork!"

A few miles down the road all of the kids started squealing, "Look, there it is!"

Daddy eased into the parking lot beside the rocking chair that seemed to get bigger and bigger the closer they got! When he stopped the car, everyone quickly jumped out. No one could believe how tiny their car looked next to the chair! Mommy said she thought it would be hard to find a rocking chair bigger than the one in Emlenton, but this one certainly was!

After admiring the mural on the building, they all went inside the general store where the owner proudly told them that many others have tried to claim that they had the largest rocking chair, but his was in the Guinness Book of World Records!

Mommy was so impressed she bought a set of souvenir mugs with the rocking chair on it for her and Daddy.

After Annie was satisfied that she had taken enough pictures, they got back into the car and continued on their way.

In Rolla, the babies started to point and giggle when they saw statues of mules beside a sign for The Mule Trading Post. When all the kids started to beg Daddy to stop, he said it WAS getting awfully hot outside and he was ready for a good, cold drink. Annie was glad she'd be able to take some photographs of the cool signs while Daddy bought the drinks.

After everyone was back in the car, Daddy said he wanted to find The Totem Pole Trading Post in Rolla because they had Route 66 gas pumps. Daddy thought it would be fun to get authentic Route 66 gas.

A few minutes later, Mommy pointed to the sign and said, "There it is!"

But when Daddy pulled up to the pumps, he was disappointed to discover they were no longer in operation. "At least the Trading Post is still open. Let's go inside," he said.

Inside, they saw a totem pole! The owner told them that it used to be outside the original store. He explained that the store used to be in a different location and moved when the Route 66 alignment changed. They knew if they were going to stay in business, they'd have to move to where the traffic was. The Mouse Family enjoyed the visit and by the time they left, they felt like they'd met another new friend.

Mommy said it was her turn to drive again. She liked driving the quieter, scenic roads. She was glad Daddy was willing to drive through the big cities, since she knew she wouldn't be comfortable with it.

In Jerome, Mommy pointed to a stone arch with the words, "Trail of Tears," across the top. Annie thought the arch was beautiful, but she didn't know what the words meant. Sam said he'd learned all about it in Social Studies and Annie would learn about it when she was older, too.

That was it! Annie had enough of hearing, "when you're older." She wanted to know NOW. There was a reason those words were on that arch and she wanted to know what it was!

Sam started to explain about how the Cherokee Indians were forced to leave their land and had to walk from their homes in the southeast to Oklahoma. Many of them died during the long journey.

Annie thought maybe Sam was right; she didn't want to hear about this now. She wasn't sure she understood. How could anyone be forced to leave their land? It sounded scary! It also made her very sad. She said she wanted to take a nap.

They were all very tired by the time they got to Lebanon. Just as they were approaching the Munger Moss Motel the neon lights came on.

Mommy said, "Look, it's the Munger Moss Motel! I saw it in our travel guide. Let's stay here tonight," as she pulled up to the office.

They were all eager to get out of the car. Daddy said that anyone who came into the office with him had to stay close by his side. Only Annie went inside with Daddy.

When they walked through the door, Annie asked Daddy, "Are you sure this is a motel? It sort of looks like a museum!"

The lady behind the counter heard Annie and laughed. She said if they were looking for the Route 66 Museum they'd have to go to the library building, which wasn't far away, but was probably closed for the evening. She said that they would even be able to see the original phones that used to be in the motel. Daddy said that could be their first stop in the morning, but right now they were looking for a motel room. Daddy was relieved when she responded that they were in luck; she only had one large room left.

The whole family slept really well that night! In the morning, when they were checking out, the nice lady was still there.

Daddy asked, "Don't you ever get off work?"

She laughed and told them that she and her husband owned the motel. "We love meeting people from all over the world and really love when families with small children come to stay and learn a little of Route 66 history."

Daddy said they'd like to see the museum she told them about the night before. With directions in hand, they all said goodbye.

Daddy had no trouble finding the library building that housed the museum. Annie would have liked to stay all day, especially since it was in the library. They all got excited when they saw the old phone system from the Munger Moss. They couldn't believe how big it was compared to the phones today. Mommy explained that an operator used to connect callers. You had to say which room number you wanted and be placed through. There was no direct dialing like there is today and no one had cell phones, either.

When they finally got back on the road, they stopped again not too far down the road in Phillipsburg.

Mommy loved antique stores and the Historic Route 66 Antique Mall looked so inviting with an old wagon and buggy out front. Daddy said these were the types of vehicles people used to get around in before the modern day automobile was invented.

Annie said, "Wow, it would take forever to get across the country in a horse-drawn wagon!"

Jenny said it was already taking forever; she couldn't imagine trying to get across the country in one of THOSE!

Once they left the Antique Mall, the thumping of the tires as they drove through empty towns put Annie to sleep. While she dozed she heard Mommy and Daddy talking about another Springfield but she just couldn't keep her eyes open! She didn't wake up until the car stopped in front of Gay Parita's Sinclair Station near Paris Springs.

When the car stopped, Annie jumped awake and asked, "Where are we? How long was I asleep? What did I miss? Why'd you let me sleep so long?" She hadn't wanted to miss any of Route 66.

Mommy explained that she missed a lot of beautiful scenery, but Daddy took the interstate through Springfield and they hadn't made any other stops.

Annie was confused. "Didn't we already drive through Springfield before?" she asked.

They all laughed and Jenny said, "Go back to sleep, Annie."

Daddy gently explained that they had already driven through Springfield in Illinois, but Missouri also had a Springfield. Mommy said she thought every state had a town called Springfield.

While they were all teasing Annie for having slept so long, a man came over to the car, introduced himself as Gary and said, "You can't see anything from there! Come on out!"

Once out of the car, Gary invited them in to see the treasures inside his garage. Annie wasn't sure what most of the things were, but she knew what root beer was and all of the children got to sit outside and have their own bottle of Route 66 Root Beer while Daddy and Gary talked a lot about the antiques in the garage. Gary

shared many stories about the old days and Annie enjoyed listening to him talk. When they were ready to leave, Gary signed their travel book with, "Friends for Life." As they were saying goodbye, Gary told them, "By the time you get home, you'll already be planning your next trip!"

"I think we already are!" Daddy replied.

They continued driving through more small towns enjoying the beautiful scenery before Daddy suddenly slammed on the brakes and stopped the car. Ahead, it looked like a little plane had crashed into the bushes! Sam read from the travel guide, "The Flying Crap Duster is the name of a folk art sculpture made from an antique manure spreader by artist Lowell Davis." They all laughed. They couldn't believe how real the person inside the plane looked[9]!

Bobby asked, "Don't you remember? Gary told us to watch out for this! We're supposed to see a village called Red Oak II near here."

Mommy pointed to the sign that showed where to turn, but Daddy said, "It looks like we have to go a little off the route to get to it. How about if we check it out on our way back home?"

Mommy agreed that they'd want to save some sites for the return trip. "Besides, we'll want to stop back and talk to Gary again, too!"

They continued talking about their visit with Gary until Daddy pulled into the parking lot of the Boots Court.

"We're not ready to get a room for the night, yet. Why are we stopping here?" Mommy asked.

"Gary told me about this place. He said we should stop and see it since the new owners did a lot of work to make it look like it did back in the 1940s. I thought it would be something for us to see."

One of the owners, Deb, proudly offered to give them a tour. While walking them to a room, she explained how they had to take the roof off in order to restore the appearance to its original design. Daddy was impressed. "Wow! That must have been a lot of work!"

---

9   Scan the code to learn more about the artist or visit http://tinyurl.com/mpq4lqx.

Inside the room, Mommy said, "I love the radio and bedspread! It reminds me of my great-grandma's house. It looks so inviting here! Maybe we could stay here on the way home."

After finishing the tour, Deb told them to be sure to visit Carthage Square. "You wouldn't want to miss seeing the Jasper County Courthouse Route 66 Museum," she said.

Daddy easily found the square and parked the car in front of the Jasper County Courthouse.

Annie felt tiny standing outside of the huge, beautiful stone building! Mommy exclaimed, "WOW! This looks like a CASTLE!"

When they went inside a nice lady offered them a ride in an old-fashioned elevator. They eagerly piled in! The lady pulled the doors closed and said, "Going up."

Mommy said her grandma had taken her in an elevator like this in downtown Youngstown, Ohio when she was a little girl.

Daddy said all elevators used to be like this with an operator who was responsible for opening and closing the doors and pushing the buttons to start and stop the elevator. The operator was responsible for the safety of the riders.

Once they got off of the elevator, they discovered the rest of the treasures within the building. There were murals that showed the history of the area and many artifacts on display.

After enjoying a walk around the square Daddy said they should be getting back on the road.

Annie settled back into her seat and asked, "What state will we go through next, Daddy?"

Daddy handed her the map and told her to see if she could discover that for herself. Annie looked at the map awhile, and then said, "I know! I've got it figured out! We'll be in Iowa- that's the next state we'll come to!"

Sam grabbed the map from her and said, "No, dummy! You're looking at the map the wrong way! We're going west, not north!"

"Daddy, Sam called me a dummy!" Annie tattled.

Daddy scolded Sam, "How many times have I told you there will be no name calling? Apologize to your sister now!"

Sam glared at Annie, then mumbled, "sorry, Annie."

Bobby took the map and said gently, "Look, Annie, we just left Carthage and we are headed west to Joplin. Always remember that west is to the left when you look at the map. Now, what is the next state we will come to when you look at the map to the left of Missouri?"

Annie liked the way Bobby talked to her. He was always more gentle than Sam. Annie looked more closely at the map and said, "I get it! We'll be in Kansas!"

Jenny suddenly shouted, "Look! There's a drive-in! Just like we saw in the Joliet Museum, only this one's real!"

Annie asked if they could see a movie at the drive-in. Daddy said the movies started to play after dark, so maybe on the way back home they could stay in the Boots Court for the night and see a movie then. Mommy said she thought that sounded like a great idea!

Daddy continued driving west, stopping at the Route 66 Visitor's Center in Webb City. Annie tripped getting out of the car and started to cry when she saw that her knee was bleeding.

Jenny said, "Geesh, Annie! What ELSE are you going to do on this trip?"

Mommy checked her bag and realized she forgot to pack Band-Aids. Daddy said he'd noticed a drug store around the corner. "I'll run over and get some."

Mommy took the children in the Visitor's Center while they waited for Daddy to return with the Band-Aids.

When Daddy came back he not only had the Band-Aids, he had a milkshake for them to share. Handing it to Annie, Daddy said, "There was a deli right across from the drugstore so I decided to check it out. I thought this might make Annie feel better." As Daddy kissed her on the forehead he added, "But you have to share with your brothers and sisters!"

"Okay, Daddy," Annie said as she took her first sip. She'd already forgotten about the cut on her knee!

As the other children came rushing toward Annie Daddy added, "And if anyone whines, they won't get any at all!"

Mommy said, "Daddy, you know we'll be in Joplin soon and we're going to stop and get pizza. Remember? Cousin Bob told us not to miss the pizza at Woody's."

Daddy said he remembered. "A few sips of a milkshake won't spoil their appetites."

Mommy glared at him but didn't say anything else. "It's time we continued on to Joplin," she said.

After everyone was satisfied they'd had their share of the milkshake, everyone piled back into the car.

Sam asked, "Wasn't Joplin destroyed in a tornado? Will there be anything left to see there?"

Daddy said that while it was true that the 2011 tornado had destroyed parts of Joplin, he'd read that nothing along Route 66 had been damaged.

In Joplin, all of the children got excited when they came upon an amusement park with a Ferris Wheel. Annie had never ridden on a Ferris Wheel before and thought it looked like fun!

"Can we stop there, please, please, please?" Sarah, Sandy, and Sally all begged in unison.

Daddy looked towards Mommy, "What do you think, Mommy?"

Mommy said if they were going to stop it would be best to do it BEFORE eating pizza.

In the park, Annie was surprised to see how high the Ferris Wheel looked once she was standing next to it. She wasn't sure she wanted to be up that high! Before the others had a chance to tease her, Daddy whispered gently, "You could sit next to me, Annie. You'll be safe."

Even though she kept her eyes squeezed shut for most of the time, Annie enjoyed the ride and was glad she'd trusted Daddy!

After a few rides in the park, they were all very hungry and ready to try Woody's Wood-Fire Pizza. They all agreed that Uncle Bob was right- this pizza WAS yummy! Annie could not believe how many special treats they were having on this trip! She had never seen Mommy look so happy!

Chapter Fourteen:
Kansas

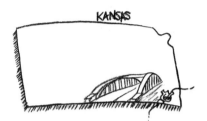

After leaving Woody's, Mommy said they'd be in Kansas in a few minutes since Joplin was the last town in Missouri.

Jenny read from the travel guide, "There are only 13 miles of Route 66 in Kansas." As she finished reading, Mommy pointed to the "Welcome to Galena" sign ahead and said, "We're in Kansas, kids!"

Just around the bend was a place called 4 Women on the Route. Daddy and Sam got excited when they saw the old, rusty tow truck alongside the building that had once been a gas station. Annie went inside with Mommy where they discovered a really cool gift shop and diner.

As they continued through Kansas, Mommy thought the Galena Museum looked really interesting but it wasn't open so Daddy kept driving towards Riverton. "Maybe we could catch it open on the way back home," Daddy said.

As the car turned around a curve in the road, Mommy let out an excited gasp as she pointed to beautiful flowers in a wagon. Mommy loved flowers! She soon realized it was a market and said, "Let's stop."

Inside, they were surprised to see that it was much more than a food market; it was also a Route 66 souvenir shop. Mommy bought some cheese for them to snack on later. Scott, the owner of the market introduced himself and told them even though the sign on the building still said Eisler Brothers, it would soon be changed to Nelson's. When they were ready to leave, Scott told them to be sure to drive over the Marsh Rainbow Bridge. He told Daddy to take the Old 66 alignment and they'd have no trouble finding it.

As they approached the bridge, Annie exclaimed, "Hey, look! It's white!" She had expected it to be painted in the colors of the rainbow.

They all wondered why it was called The Rainbow Bridge, so Jenny decided to look in the travel guide. After flipping for a few seconds she said, "Ah- I found something here!" She continued to read from the travel guide, "The bridge was designed by an engineer named James Marsh and was built around 1923. It's called Rainbow Bridge because of its shape. This is the last Marsh Bridge on Route 66- all the others have been demolished."

Daddy enjoyed driving over the bridge and Annie was excited about the pictures she took of the bridge and the Kansas Route 66 shields painted on the roadway. Sam asked if they could drive over the bridge again. Daddy thought it sounded like a great idea!

Daddy said when he looked at the map at home he thought they'd only need about a half an hour to drive through Kansas. He had no idea there would be so much to see! Daddy stopped the car in Baxter Springs and the Mouse family walked up and down the street before stopping at the Café on the Route to have a late dinner[10]. As they entered the Cafe, they read the sign on the side of the building informing them it used to be a bank and it had been robbed by Jesse James in 1876!

The kids all shouted at once, "Jesse James was here, too?!" Annie was happy she knew who Jesse James was and no one told her she would learn who he was when she was older.

At dinner, the twins started to fuss and cry. Mommy said she thought they'd had enough fun for one day. Their waitress informed them that there was still a room available upstairs in The Little Brick Inn if they needed lodging. Mommy and Daddy were very happy to hear that news! Sam thought it would be great to stay in a building that was robbed by Jesse James! "I can't wait to tell all my friends at school about THIS," he exclaimed.

Annie fell asleep as soon as her head hit the pillow! She was exhausted from all of the adventures they were having!

---

10   The Café on the Route/Little Brick Inn closed in January 2013.

Chapter Fifteen:
Oklahoma! Where the Wind Comes Sweeping Down the Plain...

Just as the sun was rising the next morning, Annie was awakened by Jenny, who was calling her name and pushing on her arm. "WHAT?" Annie shouted, groggily, as she rubbed her eyes.

Jenny replied with genuine concern in her voice, "Annie, you're moaning and yelling in your sleep! What's the matter? You're not going to be sick again, are you?"

Mommy and Daddy came running to Annie's side when they heard the commotion.

Annie felt foolish- again. She laughed, "I was dreaming about being in the bank when Jesse James came to rob it! I was so scared!"

Everyone laughed and Jenny rolled her eyes. Mommy said that since they were all awake they might as well get on the road again. Eager to continue their trip, they decided to skip a big breakfast and just have a piece of the cheese Mommy bought from the market. Mommy was pleased when all of the children pitched in to repack the car without any fussing or whining. After thanking their hostess for a wonderful stay, they were back on the road, ready for another adventure-filled day.

Only a few minutes later, they were entering Oklahoma! Mommy started to sing, "Oklahoma, where the da da da da da..."

All of the kids said in unison, "Maaaaawmeeeeeeeee!" They didn't like when she sang like that! She never could remember all the words to a song so she just filled in the tune with nonsense words.

Laughing, Mommy said it was a famous tune that she heard a long time ago but other than the name of the state sung loudly she couldn't remember the rest of the words. Mommy said that she thought the song was in a movie, too. "I'll have to remember to look for it when we get home from the trip," she said.

As they entered Quapaw, Daddy passed by a sign that said, "Entering Indian Territory." Annie was worried. "Daddy, you better go back and read the sign! What if we're not allowed to be here? We're not Indians!"

Daddy laughed and said the sign was there to give them some history of the area, but it was a great idea to go back and read it.

Daddy returned to the monument and read the sign to his family. It said that there had been 20 tribes of Indians in the area, who earned a living from mining lead and zinc. Bobby, who had been reading the travel guide, suddenly blurted out, "Here's something interesting- the name of the town is pronounced "oo-gah-paw." I never would have figured that out from looking at the spelling!"

Not far down the road, they entered the town of Commerce. Everyone was starting to get really hot and the babies were already getting fussy. The announcer on the car radio said it was already 99 degrees outside!

Daddy said it seemed like this would be a great day for taking things slow and easy! Mommy pointed to an ice cream stand and thought it would be a good time to stop for a cold treat.

Annie couldn't believe her ears! They were getting ice cream treats before lunch!

Once inside, they learned Commerce was the boyhood home of Mickey Mantle, the famous baseball player. Since Annie didn't care too much about baseball, that didn't mean anything to her, but Daddy and her brothers seemed to get really excited about that fact!

After finishing their ice cream, Daddy drove past the house where Mickey Mantle grew up before they continued their drive towards Miami. Bobby, reading from the guidebook, informed them that the name of this town is pronounced "MY-AM-UH."

Mommy said it was a good thing Bobby was telling everyone how to pronounce the names of the towns! "I thought this one would be the same as the city in Florida, since it's spelled the same."

While driving through Miami, Jenny was the first to notice the Cuckoo coming out at the top of Waylan's Ku-Ku Burger. She asked if they could stop there for lunch. They all chimed in, "Yeah, Daddy, stop there, please Daddy?" Even Mommy thought it sounded like a great idea.

Daddy said, "It looks like we're going to eat our way through today!" They all giggled as Daddy pulled into the parking lot.

After finishing their burgers and fries, they all agreed it was a great stop! On full bellies, they proceeded through Miami, finally stopping in front of a beautiful white building. Daddy wondered what it was. "It looks so magnificent, I'm curious about it," he said.

The doors to the Coleman Theater were open and a woman in the entry invited them in to see the theater. She said there would be a show later in the evening, but she would be happy to show them around. Mommy couldn't believe their good fortune! They were going to have a guided tour of the building. Daddy reminded the children not to touch anything and to stay together.

Annie felt her cheeks get red as she remembered getting lost in the flea market. She wasn't about to leave Mommy and Daddy's side again! Out on the stage, Annie wondered what it would be like to stand in front of an audience and perform. She was so shy; she thought she would pass out if she ever had to do anything like that!

Once in the car, Daddy said, "I guess you never know what treasures you're going to find out on Route 66!" He turned the corner, following the signs for "Old Route 66" and soon found himself driving on what looked like a sidewalk! Daddy asked, "Did I miss a sign? Was I supposed to turn somewhere?"

Bobby read from the travel guide, "The Sidewalk Highway is only nine feet wide and is part of the Ozark Trail." The road was very bumpy and Daddy had to drive very carefully. It hadn't rained in a while and the roadway was very dry and dusty. Dust was surrounding the car. Daddy could hardly see in front of him! He said, "I hope nobody comes down this road heading east! We'll be meeting them if they do!"

Once off of the historic Sidewalk Highway, Daddy stopped the car at the Afton Station Packard Museum. Daddy, who loved old cars, went with the older kids to look at the car collection, while Mommy, Annie and the younger kids stayed in the gift shop and talked to Laurel. There were many old signs and postcards to look at. Annie was curious about a sign that said "Burma Shave" and Laurel explained it was a shaving cream company that advertised by putting up clever sayings with a few words on each sign that travelers would read as they drove down the road[11].

Mommy handed Annie a post card, "Look at this. It's a photograph of a Burma Shave sign from along the old road."

Annie read the signs on the card out loud: "Why is it when you try to pass the guy in front goes twice as fast Burma Shave."

Once Daddy returned from looking at the cars, Mommy paid for the postcard and other souvenirs. Before leaving, Laurel asked them to sign her guest book. Annie was glad she had practiced writing her name in cursive so she could sign her name like Daddy did instead of printing like a little kid.

After leaving Afton Station they saw many abandoned buildings and cars. Annie thought the stone buildings were beautiful and it made her sad to see them abandoned. Daddy said it made him sad to see the old cars left to rust out in the fields.

They drove on in silence for a long time before seeing signs for the World's Largest Totem Pole in Foyil. They all agreed it was someplace they'd like to stop, even though they would have to travel

---

11   Scan the code for more information about the Burma-Shave company and its signs or visit http://tinyurl.com/2wswxa.

four miles off of Route 66. As they pulled into the parking lot, they were surprised to see there were many totem poles in Ed Galloway's Totem Pole Park. Mommy said, "I thought we were only going to drive past one totem pole, but it looks like we're going to have to get out of the car to see them all."

Even though there were many totem poles in the park, the world's largest, at 90 feet tall, was Annie's favorite. Little Sister Sandy said she couldn't even see the top! All the kids enjoyed running around the totem poles and chasing each other in the grass before getting back in the car. Mommy said the little ones needed to have stops like this to keep them from getting fussy.

By the time they got to Claremore, Buster and Billy were sound asleep. Mommy suggested they save touring Claremore for their trip back home. Bobby, who was still reading from the travel guide, said it looked like there was a lot to see and do in Claremore, the home of Will Rogers.

Jenny asked, "Who was Will Rogers?"

Bobby continued reading from the travel guide, "Will Rogers was a famous American cowboy and an entertainer in the 1920s and 1930s. He was born in the Indian territory that is now Oklahoma and was very famous. He is known as Oklahoma's favorite son."

Mommy said, "I guess that's why we keep seeing signs for the Will Rogers Highway."

Bobby changed the subject. "I found something else in the travel guide that looks like fun. Can we wake the twins up when we get to Catoosa? I think they'd want to see the Blue Whale Swimming Park."

"A swimming park? Oh, THAT sounds like fun," Annie exclaimed.

The others quickly agreed and began excitedly talking about what they would do once they got there. There was no need to worry about having to wake the twins up. By the time Daddy parked the car, the boys woke up from all of the noisy chatter, wondering where they were.

They were all disappointed to learn that swimming was no longer permitted. But they were excited to discover they were able to walk inside and explore the whale itself. It was huge! A sign said it was 80 feet long! Annie loved to swim and thought it must have been a lot of fun to come here when it was still open for swimming. Mommy said she could imagine the crowds that must have come here "back in the day."

Back in the car, Daddy again got confused by road signs and ended up on the turnpike, going around Tulsa. Daddy was relieved when, instead of getting upset with him, Mommy said, "Oh well, one more city to see on our return trip home!"

Cars and trucks were passing by their station wagon so fast Annie started to get dizzy watching them before she remembered Mommy's advice to only look out of the front window. Daddy was going much slower than most of the other cars on the road. He got off of the turnpike as soon as he could! He liked the slower pace of Route 66.

Annie liked that she could take more pictures as they drove through the small towns. She wasn't able to take any pictures at all when they were on the interstate! She took many pictures as they drove through Sapulpa, Bristow, Depew and Stroud. They didn't stop again until they were ready to eat dinner in Davenport.

Mommy excitedly pointed to the sign for Seaba Station in Warwick. Her guidebook said it was an antique store. But when Daddy pulled into the parking lot, they discovered it was closed and in the middle of being turned into a motorcycle museum. Daddy thought it might even be open on their return trip home. He and Sam thought a motorcycle museum would be even better to see than an antique store! Mommy said she wasn't so sure about THAT, but Daddy could stop again on the way home if he wanted to.

Before driving away, they all took a peak inside the "restroom" building that Daddy called an "outhouse." They all agreed they were happy to have a real bathroom in their home!

Annie took a picture of a "Welcome to Wellston" mural as they drove through that town. She loved seeing the artwork on the buildings.

Bobby wondered if they could paint murals on some of the old buildings in their town when they got home. Mommy suggested that he talk to his art teacher at school about turning that into a class project. Bobby thought that sounded like a great idea!

As they entered Arcadia, they saw a barn with a car coming out of the side of it! Sam had their travel guide and said, "This must be John Hargrove's Route 66 Museum. Can we stop there, Daddy? It's supposed to be filled with stuff from all over Route 66."

Daddy agreed and several hours later they were glad they'd stopped! Annie was excited that John let her sit in the driver's seat of the car that looked like it was going through the building.

John told them that many of the things they were seeing on his property were replicas of things they would find as they continued their journey.

As they were leaving, John advised them to be sure to stop at the Round Barn down the road. "You've got to go inside to really appreciate it. Don't just drive by!"

John was right! They definitely didn't want to miss this unique barn! The ceiling was a spectacular design. It was huge and seemed to go high into the sky! Annie felt very tiny inside.

A guide gave them a tour of the building and explained how it was rebuilt by volunteers. They learned that old fashioned barn dances used to be held upstairs. Mommy and Daddy even waltzed all the way around the dance floor one time! Annie had never seen her Mommy giggling like THAT before!

Arcadia had a lot of fun things to see. Not too far down the road from the Round Barn, they saw a huge soda pop bottle in front of a business called "POPS." They were all curious to find out what was inside. They learned the huge bottle sculpture was 66 feet high and changed colors at night. The windows displayed all kinds of soda pop in many colors and flavors. The Mouse family never drank pop at home and Annie said she had no idea it came in so many colors! Daddy said since it was a special occasion they could all choose one bottle. Since Annie's favorite color was blue, she chose a blue bottle. Jenny chose red and Sam chose green. All of the others chose root beer. As they sat in the diner and drank their bottles of pop, Jenny giggled and pointed at Annie. "Look at Annie! Her tongue and lips are blue!"

Sam teased, "Hey, Jenny, what are you laughing about? Your lips and tongue are bright red!"

Bobby added, "Uh- Sam- have you looked in the mirror? Your

tongue is green!"

This sent them all into giggles. Annie wanted to see what she looked like, so Mommy took out her mirror. Bobby was disappointed that his root beer didn't turn his lips or tongue into a bright color, too. "If we get another chance to have pop, I want to get a bright color that turns my tongue a funny color, too."

Daddy noticed that others were watching them as the children got louder and louder with their giggling. He looked at his watch and said, "OK, kids, time to settle down. Let's finish up here so we could go on to Oklahoma City."

The children continued laughing and talking about all of the different pop colors while piling back into the car. As they drove through Oklahoma City, they noticed many buildings with stone that Annie thought looked like giraffes! Sally asked, "Do you think there's a pop color that could turn your tongue into a giraffe, Annie?"

They finally stopped giggling when Annie asked if Daddy would stop the car so she could take a picture of Owl Court. Bobby read from their travel guide that it used to be a popular Route 66 motel but had been closed for quite some time. He also discovered that the buildings that looked like giraffes were built out of Ozark sandstone.

Buster pointed up in the sky and said, "milk, milk." Annie started to reach for a bottle out of the cooler, believing Buster wanted milk. Jenny said, "No. Look up in the sky! There's a giant milk bottle on that building!" They all laughed and Annie reached for her camera. Annie was glad Daddy had to stop at a red light so she was able to snap a picture of it from the car window.

Annie had one more surprise in Oklahoma City- a diner called, Ann's Fry House! Mommy thought it seemed like the perfect place to stop and eat. Annie agreed, since she wanted to take a picture of the cool cars parked in the front. There was so much to see both outside and inside and the food was great, too!

When they got to El Reno Mommy pointed to a sign for the Cherokee Trading Post and said, "Let's go in there. I'd like to see the Native American arts and crafts."

Mommy warned all of the children that they were to stay by her side and were not to touch ANYTHING inside the store.

As soon as they walked inside they heard music coming from

the back of the store. Mommy thought it was the most beautiful sound she had ever heard and began to walk to where the music was coming from. She saw a man playing a wooden flute with an eagle on it.

Mommy and the children watched him as he played. When he stopped playing, he placed a new mouthpiece on it and handed the flute to Mommy. "Here, you try it."

Mommy said, "I don't know how to play a flute! I've never even held one!"

Annie said, "Mommy, go ahead and try it!"

The triplets all chimed in, "Yeah, Mommy, try it!"

The man showed Mommy how to hold the flute and showed her what to do. Mommy followed his instructions and couldn't believe the beautiful sound that came out! She played a few more notes before handing the flute back to the man.

Everyone agreed that Mommy seemed to have a natural talent for playing the flute.

Daddy asked Mommy, "Would you like that flute for your special souvenir?"

Mommy was very excited when she replied, "I'd LOVE it!" Daddy said, "Then it's yours." He told the man to wrap it up for her.

"It sounds so calming. I think you should play it at bedtime to help the children fall asleep," Daddy said as he handed the package to Mommy.

Annie said she'd like to hear that music playing as she was trying to fall asleep. The rest of the children agreed.

Mommy kissed Daddy on the cheek and added, "I'd love to play this for all of you every night right after your bedtime story."

Sam read a sign that identified items that were made by the local Native Americans of the Cherokee tribe. The shop attendant explained that stores were required to let people know which items were authentic Native American items and which items were not. He then pointed to some drums he thought they would be interested in seeing. He picked one up and said with pride in his voice, "I know the family that makes these drums. They are perfect for children! Listen!" He then beat out a rhythm. The sound was beautiful.

Bobby stood watching and listening. Finally, he asked, "Daddy, THAT'S what I would like for my special souvenir. Could I get one?"

"I think that's a great choice, son," Daddy answered.

Mommy wasn't so sure. She asked, "Daddy, have you thought about the noise the children will be making on that thing the rest of the trip?"

Daddy replied, "Don't worry about it. How many chances will they get for a trip like this?"

Mommy just rolled her eyes. She knew there was no use in arguing with him, but she wondered what he would think in a few hours! Bobby picked out a drum that he said was "perfect." Mommy reminded him that he could not ask for another souvenir during the rest of the trip.

Mommy turned just in time to see the triplets about to knock over a bin filled with brightly colored stones. "Girls! What did I tell you about touching things in here? Daddy, I think it's time we leave."

As they were walking back to the car, Annie wished she had spoken up and asked for a drum, too. But she was afraid to spend her money too soon. She had been looking at some of the pretty stones and crystals. She had never seen any that looked like that in Pennsylvania. Maybe Daddy would stop back here on the way home if she hadn't spent her money by the time they came back this way.

Back in the car, Jenny tried to pull the drum off of Bobby. "Let me see it! Don't be selfish!" She reached over to pull it off of him.

Bobby held on tight. "No, it's mine! You could have gotten your own."

Jenny crossed her arms, then stuck her tongue out at Bobby. "Keep your stupid drum! I don't like it anyway," she said angrily.

Bobby started to beat out a tune. Mommy and Daddy yelled at the same time, "BOBBY! NOT IN THE CAR!"

Jenny looked at Bobby and snickered, "Ha ha, you got in trouble!"

The triplets all started to giggle loudly- in unison.

Daddy said angrily, "Do I have to turn this car around and go back home? Do you want to forget about the Grand Canyon?"

They all quieted down quickly! Bobby put his drum under the seat. Mommy said she thought it was a great time for the children to take a nap so she could read her travel guide in peace!

Annie didn't feel like napping; when she did, she missed recording the names of the towns in her journal and she didn't want to miss ANYTHING! But she knew she better keep quiet or Daddy might turn the car back around and they'd never see the Grand Canyon!

Just past Hydro, Daddy stopped the car in front of what looked like a gas station. But this one wasn't open for business anymore. "Lucille's" was restored to honor the owner of the gas station, Lucille Hamons, who was known as "The Mother of the Mother Road." Bobby read from the travel guide and told them it said that people who were traveling west on Route 66 to look for work would often have their cars break down or run out of money. Lucille helped anyone in need who stopped at her place and that's how she got her nickname. Bobby continued reading from the travel guide that Lucille's Roadhouse was a restaurant built to look like the gas station and it was only a few miles down the road in Weatherford.

A few minutes later, Annie and Jenny shouted at the same time, "There it is, Daddy!"

Daddy turned to Mommy and asked, "Shall we stop and eat?"

Mommy nodded in agreement. "Let's sit at the counter. Remember how much fun we used to have spinning on the seats at the counter in the old five and dime before we had kids?"

Annie was excited that they got to sit at the counter while they ate their burgers and fries and sipped on their milkshakes. They were stuffed by the time they left! Everyone agreed that it was a great stop!

As they approached Clinton, Sam pointed to the huge sign for the Oklahoma Route 66 museum. Daddy asked if they would like to go in and see it. Wow! Another treat! Annie was excited! Jenny rolled her eyes, but didn't say anything. She didn't get as excited about museums as Annie did, but she had to admit, they were seeing some pretty cool things that she had never seen before.

Once inside, they had a chance to see what Route 66 was like before Interstate 40 was built, when so many small towns existed to provide services to the travelers and tourists passing through. They could see how different life was for the people who lived along the old route. They also understood why all of the businesses closed up, too. As the cars flew by on the interstate, they didn't have any reason to go through the small towns. They didn't need to stay as many nights in hotels as they once needed to while making their way across the country, either. With little business, people moved out of the towns to find work, so all of the homes were left empty, too. Slowly, the once thriving towns were left empty.

They also learned about the "Dust Bowl Days" of the 1930s, which was caused by both a severe drought and poor farming techniques. The Mouse family learned the dust storms were as bad as the snow blizzards in Pennsylvania, but the dust storms lasted for years. Thinking about the people who lost their homes and businesses made Annie feel sad.

There were many things that made Annie and her brothers and sisters laugh, too. Annie said, "Oh look! There are more of those Burma Shave signs like we saw in Afton Station!"

Mommy pointed to an old wagon loaded up with what she said was 'everything they owned" as they tried to escape the dust storms.

They also saw an old fashioned soda fountain on display. Annie wished they had one of those in her town. Mommy said they used to a long time ago and she used to go there with her friends after school. Daddy said it wasn't just the towns along Route 66 that changed; all the small towns across America have changed since he and Mommy were kids. Mommy said that back then everyone knew their neighbors and looked out for each other.

The exit of the museum led to the gift shop. It had replicas of the old cars that used to cruise by on Route 66. Daddy saw a replica of a 1959 pink Cadillac. "Well, I just found MY special souvenir," he exclaimed.

With Sam being the oldest child and first son, he always liked to do everything Daddy did. He wanted to get his souvenir from this museum, too. Sam asked Daddy if he could buy a replica of a Harley Davidson motorcycle. He thought it would be cool to drive a motorcycle some day.

Mommy glared, "I don't want to hear any talk about motorcycles."

Sam put it back and decided to wait to buy something he really wanted.

On the way out the door Daddy noticed the old diner beside the museum. Mommy just looked at Daddy and said, "Are you serious? You want to EAT again!"

Daddy laughed and said, "You can't eat here, it's part of the museum display!"

They learned that the diner on display was called a "Valentine Diner," named after the man who started the chain of tiny counter-service diners.

Sarah, Sandy and Sally wanted to go inside. They wanted to know if they could spin around on the stools at the counter, like they'd just done at Lucille's. Bobby tried to open the door but it was locked. Mommy said they were only allowed to walk around the outside and look inside through the glass.

Once they finally got out of the parking lot, they continued along Route 66 until they came to Foss Park. Bobby liked the small jail they saw in Gardner, Illinois and wondered what the jail in Foss looked like. This one resembled a cage. It was 105 degrees outside and Daddy said he couldn't imagine being locked in that thing outside in this kind of heat!

Bobby, reading from their travel guide, said there was another tiny jail in Canute and wondered if they could stop and see that one, too. He wondered if they were all made the same in Oklahoma or if they would be different.

Daddy said, "Let's go find out!"

They were all surprised to see that the one in Canute looked more like a storage building in someone's yard. They didn't stop and go inside.

As they approached Elk City, they saw signs for a National Route 66 museum. Mommy said it was too soon to stop at another museum, and Daddy agreed. But once they saw the huge Kachina statue out front the children begged Daddy to stop! This museum looked like an entire village.

Once inside, all of the kids started to run in different directions.

Annie rushed to go sit inside a car with a television screen to see what it felt like to travel along Route 66 in the olden days. Mommy and Daddy had to remind everyone to stay together and there would be NO RUNNING inside the building. Daddy asked if they would like to leave this minute in that voice he used when he meant business. They quickly all came back to Mommy and Daddy and waited patiently to explore the museum together. There was so much to see that they stayed until the museum closed. While walking back to the car, they noticed a park right across the street. It even had a carousel!

The twins began to cry. Mommy and Daddy realized it was way past dinnertime. Daddy suggested getting some carryout food and eating in the park. Mommy pointed to a picnic table and said, "Great idea! You go get the food, Daddy, and I'll wait for you over there with the children. We can have a picnic style dinner!"

No one minded waiting for Daddy to return with the food. They were all enjoying riding on the carousel!

"Wow! Another special ride AND another picnic," Annie thought. She loved having picnics. When she was the youngest, before her little brothers and sisters were born, Mommy served picnic lunches under the oak tree all the time. After the little ones were born Mommy never had time for picnics any more. Now a picnic was a real treat! They were having so many treats on this trip that it made up for being squished in the back seat of the car with her brothers and sisters.

After their picnic was over, they all piled back into the car. Just as Daddy was about to pull out of the parking lot, Annie yelled, "WAIT! Daddy, stop! I forgot to take a picture of the Kachina! Please stop! It'll only take a second."

Daddy stopped the car when he realized how important it was to her. Annie said she didn't even have to get out of the car; she could get a great picture right there just by rolling the window down. It was Daddy's turn to say, "Wait, Annie." He pulled the car back into a parking spot and told Annie to get out and sit in front of the statue. Daddy took Annie's camera and gently fixed the bow in her hair before snapping a picture of her. Annie knew this would be her favorite picture from the entire trip.

Afterwards, in the motel, they all talked about what a wonderful day they'd had. Annie asked if they would still be in Oklahoma the next day. Daddy replied they were almost through Oklahoma and would spend the next day in Texas. Mommy was just about to comment on how well the children behaved all day when Little Sister Sally wanted to know if they would be at the Grand Canyon the next day.

Jenny just sighed. "No, stupid! Didn't you hear Daddy say we were only making it to Texas tomorrow?"

Sally asked, "Isn't that where the Grand Canyon is?"

Jenny rolled her eyes and sighed deeply again.

Sally began to cry. Annie pleaded, "Leave her alone. She hasn't learned that in school yet. She doesn't know the same things we know yet." She didn't like when Jenny teased the little ones.

It was Mommy's turn to sigh deeply. Then she ordered, "Everyone to bed! NOW!"

Everyone was more than ready to go to bed. Annie fell asleep thinking about how much she loved her family, even if they did fight and argue at times, she was happy to be sharing this adventure with all of them.

The next morning, with everyone rested and eager to continue exploring Route 66, the children had no trouble listening to Mommy as they loaded up into the station wagon bright and early.

Annie was looking through the travel guide as the car rumbled along. Suddenly, she blurted out, "Sally, I know why you thought the Grand Canyon was in Texas! It says here the Palo Duro Canyon is known as the Grand Canyon of Texas!"

Sally reached under the seat and pulled out a brochure for the Palo Duro Canyon and handed it to Annie.

"No wonder you thought the Grand Canyon was in Texas, Sally! Where'd you get this?"

"Found it at the travel center. Thought it was for the Grand Canyon." Sally mumbled.

"Let me see it," Mommy ordered. Annie passed the brochure up to Mommy.

Mommy seemed impressed with what she saw. She asked, "Daddy, what do you think? Should we stop at the Grand Canyon of Texas or go all the way to Arizona?

All the kids yelled, "Arizona! We wanna go to Arizona!"

Daddy laughed, "Arizona it is! But first, let's stop and see what this is." They were now in Texola and Daddy was pointing to a small, block building.

Sam and Bobby exclaimed, "Cool! Another jail! Let's have a look!"

Exploring the Texola jail would be their last stop before crossing into Texas. It was as tiny as the others. Mommy admitted she would be claustrophobic in one of those! Annie asked what THAT meant and Mommy explained it was a fear of being in tiny, closed-in places.

Annie said she figured she'd be claustrophobic, too, and was afraid to go inside. Daddy reassured her he would hold the door open while she looked in, so she wouldn't be frightened.

The moment Annie walked in, Sam grabbed the door from Daddy, saying he'd hold it, but then acted like he was going to slam it shut. Annie began to cry and Daddy scolded Sam.

Sam said he was just having fun with Annie and wasn't REALLY going to slam the door shut.

Daddy asked sternly, "Should I head back to Pennsylvania today?"

ALL the kids began to cry, "No Daddy, we still haven't seen the Grand Canyon!"

Sam apologized quickly; he didn't want to ruin everyone's trip.

Driving out of Texola, Daddy commented on how it looked like so many of the homes were abandoned. Mommy responded that it was a shame since some of the houses looked so beautiful. Mommy said it must have been hard for people to leave their homes.

Annie was confused. From the rearview mirror, Daddy could see the look on Annie's face and asked her what she was thinking about. She answered, "Our school always asks for donations for the homeless shelter during the holidays. How come there are homeless people when there are so many empty houses?"

No one could answer her. They all got very quiet as they thought about it.

Chapter Sixteen:
The Texas Panhandle

They crossed the border into Texas. Not long after that, Jenny shouted, "Look, there's a leprechaun on top of that sign that says "Welcome to Shamrock" and I saw it first!!"

Annie was surprised to see Jenny sound so excited about something. She usually tried to pretend that she was bored or irritated, but it looked to Annie like Jenny was really excited and couldn't hide it this time.

Jenny asked Annie, "Remember the time you got lost searching for the leprechauns guarding the pot of gold at the end of the rainbow?"

Everyone laughed and Annie just hung her head, remembering how upset she had been when she didn't find the end of the rainbow OR the pot of gold and then couldn't even find her way back home! She wanted to change the topic quickly! Annie should have known the reason Jenny was so excited had something to do with poking fun at her.

Soon, they all had something else to talk about when they saw a building with two towers shooting up into the sky. One of the towers had the word "Café" on it and the other said "CONOCO" so they thought it was a gas station and a restaurant. They quickly learned that, although the building had once served both food and gasoline, it was now the Shamrock Chamber of Commerce building. Mommy and Daddy picked up some more travel brochures while Annie took more pictures. She couldn't wait to show her friend, Molly Mole, all of the fun things she'd seen on her trip! She quickly forgot all about Jenny's teasing.

As the car pulled away from the building, Annie had just finished settling into her groove on the seat when she heard a loud bang.

They all jumped! It sounded like someone shot the car! The twins began to cry and Annie and Jenny just looked at each other with fear in their eyes. Daddy eased the car to the side of the road.

Annie wailed, "Daddy, don't stop the car! Someone's shooting at us!"

Daddy did not look happy as he opened the car door. He reassured them they had not been shot at. "It sounds like I just blew a tire," he grumbled. Moments later, with his prediction confirmed, he ordered all of them out of the car so he could change the tire.

Mommy said she'd walk back to the Chamber building with the children so they wouldn't be standing on the roadway. Trying to make the most of their misfortune, she said, "Come on, kids, let's go for a walk. We could use a stretch." Sam said he'd stay with Daddy to help change the tire.

As they started walking, Mommy insisted that the children stay close to her. "Everyone take someone else's hand," she ordered. The Chamber building was still in sight and she hadn't thought it looked like a very long walk, but after a few minutes, Mommy's arms were aching from holding the twins. It was much hotter than she'd realized and they were kicking up the dry dirt from the side of the road as they walked. Annie began to cough; she whined about the dirt getting in her throat. A truck flew past them, kicking up a cloud of dust. Sarah, Sandy and Sally looked at their dust-covered clothes and started to cry.

Suddenly Mommy thought the Chamber building seemed very far away. She didn't think she could walk another inch. Her feet felt like lead, sweat was pouring down her face and her mouth was dry. She realized she should not have left the car without a bottle of water. What started out to be a nice walk down the road now seemed like a very bad idea! Mommy didn't want the children to realize she was frightened. But she wondered, in desperation, "What should I do? The car is just as far away as the Chamber building! The kids are crying and the babies are too little to put down."

Bobby and Jenny were walking just a few steps ahead of her, when Bobby pointed to something on the edge of the roadway and exclaimed, "Look, everyone!" There, growing in a crack in the asphalt was a tiny yellow flower. The kids were amazed that a flower could grow like that! Seeing the flower lifted Mommy's spirits. While the children admired the flower in awe, Mommy noticed a small clearing on the side of the road just ahead.

"Kids, let's go sit down in the grass over there," she said, while pointing to the area.

The kids ran to where Mommy pointed and plopped down in exhaustion. Mommy sighed with relief as she set Buster and Billy down. The triplets shook the dust off of their clothes. Ten minutes later, they were all relieved when Daddy pulled up in the car to get them. They ran to the car, eager to get bottles of water from the cooler.

While handing Mommy a water bottle, Daddy said, "No wonder we were all so thirsty- I just heard on the radio that it's 120 degrees outside!"

After a long drink from her water bottle, Mommy gave Daddy a kiss on the cheek. She whispered that she had never been so relieved to see him! Daddy saw the fear in her eyes and gave her hand a squeeze. He suggested they not leave each other again throughout the trip.

Finally, with the tire fixed and everyone back in their seats, they were able to continue along their way.

Entering McLean they saw a huge sign that read RATTLESNAKES! Sam and Bobby gasped. Mommy reassured, "Don't worry, kids; we won't be stopping THERE!" Everyone breathed a sigh of relief!

Not far down the street they came upon the Devil's Rope Museum and Route 66 Visitor's Center. A big sign on the building announced: TRIBUTE TO BARBED WIRE. Since the Mouse family lived on a farm, they all knew what barbed wire was, but none of them had ever heard it called "devil's rope" before. Inside, they couldn't believe all of the sculptures made out of barbed wire! Annie's favorite was the cowboy hat. Bobby thought it should be called an art museum!

In the gift shop, Mommy bought a cookbook and some Route 66 playing cards and said they could play a game in the motel later. Daddy bought a chunk of the original Texas Route 66. They all agreed that The Devil's Rope Museum was another great stop!

As he drove through McLean, Daddy excitedly pointed to the bright orange, old-fashioned gas pumps from a restored Philips 66 service station at the end of the block. The tiny building looked like a cottage. He said it reminded him of the one his father owned when Daddy was a little boy.

Daddy got very quiet and no one said anything while they all thought about their grandfather. Then Sally asked, "Daddy, why can't we go to heaven to see grandpa? I miss him!" No one answered her.

Annie wished their grandpa could be here, sharing this vacation with them. She began snapping pictures through the open window.

Annie settled back into her spot on the seat as the car moved slowly forward. As they approached the General Store and Post Office in Alanreed, a strong gust of wind sent tumbleweed flying into the air and onto the windshield! Daddy was so startled by it, he swerved the car and almost went off the side of the road. Feeling shaken, he suggested they stop at the General Store for a few minutes.

Bobby pointed to the cage alongside the building. All the kids went to explore while Mommy and Daddy went into the store to buy more drinks to restock the cooler.

"Sam and Bobby, you're in charge of looking after the others for a few minutes," Daddy ordered.

As they examined what turned out to be another tiny jail, Bobby commented that maybe the threat of being locked in one of those kept people from committing crimes. Sam agreed that no one could live very long locked up outside in one of those in this heat!

Mommy and Daddy appeared holding cartons of soda and water a few minutes later. With the cooler restocked, Mommy suggested she give Daddy a break and take another turn driving.

As they approached Groom, Annie and Jenny both pointed to a leaning water tower and started to argue over who saw it first.

Mommy snapped, "It doesn't matter who saw it first! Stop bickering already!"

Since Annie wanted Mommy to pull over so she could get a picture, she knew she'd better listen! As Annie snapped her pictures, Sam read from the travel guide that it wasn't a real water tower at all. It had been built like that to advertise a truck stop.

Daddy remarked, "I guess that would get people's attention!"

Driving through Groom, Mommy pointed to a grocery store. "Look! It looks just like the one in our town! Let's stop and get some snacks." Mommy eased into a parking spot at the curb and they all got out. As they approached the door, Daddy reminded the children to stay together. They knew he meant business when he said they weren't to touch a thing!

As soon as they entered the store, the cashier smiled and asked "Is there anything I could help y'all find?" Mommy answered they'd like some fresh fruit and the kind woman pointed to the back of the store.

Daddy said he'd stay up front with the kids while Mommy picked out the snacks. The cashier asked, "Where y'all from? Y'all don't sound like you're from Texas!"

Annie giggled and Daddy answered, "Pennsylvania." Annie said she'd never heard anyone talk the way she did, either. They all laughed together. She continued asking questions, "Y'all been drivin' since Pennsylvania?!"

She and Daddy continued talking and the Mouse family learned she was the owner of the store. Annie liked her; she treated them like they were friends even though they'd just met. She thought it was wonderful that Mommy and Daddy were taking their children on a Route 66 trip and told them to be sure to stop in Conway to see Bug Ranch.

Annie and Jenny looked at each other and said, "EWWWWW, we don't want to see any bugs!" She just laughed and reassured them that they'd enjoy seeing THESE bugs.

As they walked back to the car, Annie shouted, "Look!" as she pointed to a HUGE cross high up in the sky. As they piled back into the car, they all agreed they'd never seen a cross THAT big!

Annie announced that she would rather stay in the car when they got to Bug Ranch. For once, Jenny agreed with her! But when they got there, the "bugs" turned out to be old Volkswagen cars sticking up out of the ground, like they had been planted there!

Bobby looked it up in the travel guide and informed them this was a type of sculpture and they were allowed to use cans of spray paint to write their names on the cars. Annie and Jenny quickly changed their minds and eagerly hopped out of the car so they could explore the "bugs."

Annie said, "Too bad we don't have any spray paint cans with us."

Sam and Bobby pointed to the cans of spray paint left on the ground. Sam said, "I guess we could use these. Are we allowed to, Daddy?"

When Daddy nodded his approval, Bobby handed Annie a can of paint. She was proud of the way she painted "Annie Mouse" in cursive on a yellow car.

On the way to Amarillo, Daddy saw signs for a free 72 ounce steak at The Big Texan and decided he'd like to stop for lunch. Mommy thought it was too early to have lunch, so she suggested they stop at several antique stores and art galleries along Route 66.

As they drove through Amarillo they saw several horses standing alone on street corners. Daddy was just about to comment on how odd it was that the horses didn't have riders, when he realized that they were statues! Everyone laughed.

When they finally got to The Big Texan they saw that EVERYTHING was big at The Big Texan! There was a huge cowboy sign high up in the sky, a huge cowboy boot and a huge dining room! The waitress explained you only got the steak free if you could eat it all. She pointed to a plate with the steak on it at a table next to them, exclaiming, "That's what it looks like. Do you think you want one?"

Daddy's shoulders slumped and he muttered under his breath, "So THAT'S what 72 ounces looks like?!"

Mommy laughed and said she didn't think the entire family could eat one of those steaks! Even though they decided against the 72 ounce steak, it was still a fun place to eat. They even got to keep the menus and plastic cups as souvenirs!

After leaving The Big Texan, Mommy took over driving again.

In no time, Mommy was stopping the car in front of 6th Street Antiques in Amarillo's historic district. Daddy laughed and said Mommy ALWAYS found antique stores when she was driving!

She replied, "Just like you can always find old cars to admire!"

Daddy had to admit Mommy had a point!

Inside, Mommy was excited when she found a small pitcher just like the one she had broken many years ago. She said it was her favorite and she didn't think she'd ever find a replacement for it! The owner wrapped it carefully for her so it wouldn't break.

Jenny said she didn't understand what the big deal was about a pitcher and Mommy explained it had been a wedding gift from her grandmother. It had been very special to her.

Jenny put her head down and said quietly, "I think I understand. Just like the doll that grandpa gave me before he died is special to me."

Surprised, Annie asked, "Is that why you won't let me play with it, Jenny?" Jenny nodded her head. Annie had thought Jenny was just being mean to her when she wouldn't let her play with her doll, but now she understood.

Daddy was very happy Mommy had finally found her pitcher. He hoped Mommy wouldn't want to stop in so many antique shops now!

When they left the antique store, the owner told them not to miss Cadillac Ranch. They knew by now that whenever someone told them to be sure to see something, they should be sure to see it!

Annie could not believe her eyes when they pulled up in front of Cadillac Ranch! There were MORE cars planted in the ground! Only these cars were in the middle of a pasture and there were cows roaming between them. Annie asked, "Daddy does everybody in Texas plant their cars when they don't drive them anymore?"

Mommy laughed and told Annie this was a form of art and they were allowed to paint their names on these cars, too. Annie was a little nervous about the cows. She wondered if they were friendly like the ones on their farm. Daddy said he felt certain the cows wouldn't bother them. "I'm sure they're used to people walking through the pasture to see the cars."

After they finished painting on the cars, Sam challenged the other kids to a race back to the car and took off running. Annie and her brothers and sisters took off after him, giggling and yelling, "No fair, you got a head start, you didn't wait for us to start!"

Annie enjoyed running through the pasture after sitting in the car for so long and having to stay close to Mommy and Daddy each time they got out of the car. They arrived back to the car out of breath and laughing, with Mommy and Daddy not far behind.

Continuing on Route 66, they all burst into giggles when they suddenly saw boots hanging from a tree. They learned this was Dot's Mini Museum in Vega. It wasn't open so they couldn't go inside, but Annie was happy with the pictures she was able to take outside of the museum. Daddy said Texas sure did have a lot of quirky things to see. Annie said Texas had a lot of FUN things that she couldn't wait to share with her friend, Molly!

Annie exclaimed, "I think my camera is the best present I've ever received! I'll be able to share everything with Molly when we get back home!"

Mommy was still driving when they came to a sign in Adrian that announced they were at the midpoint of the route. Both Los Angeles and Chicago were 1139 miles away.

"Wow! That means we've already gone over a thousand miles!" Bobby exclaimed.

Jenny said, "THAT means we still have over a thousand miles to go!"

Sarah, Sandy and Sally asked, "Are we almost there?"

Pointing across the street, Daddy said, "We're almost THERE."

Daddy was pointing to The Midpoint Café right across the street from the sign. Sam read from the guidebook that this Café was known for its pies.

Even though they still all felt pretty full from their big lunch at The Big Texan, none of them wanted to pass up the opportunity for a piece of pie!

Once inside there was so much to see and so many signs to read that all of the kids got excited. Annie ran in one direction, pointing, "Look over here! This looks like one of those Burma Shave signs like we saw in the Oklahoma Route 66 museum!"

Jenny ran towards the gift shop and the triplets followed. Sam hollered, "Hey, did you see these cars?"

Daddy was afraid they would be asked to leave. In his sternest voice he called, "Stop, everyone sit down over here, NOW!"

All of the kids immediately joined Mommy and Daddy at a table and sat down. No one wanted to start for home now! Daddy made all of the children apologize for their poor behavior when the waitress came over to their table.

The waitress said the owner would be happy to see the children so excited but agreed with Daddy that running in a restaurant could be dangerous.

Annie felt ashamed. She was careful to be on her best behavior the rest of the time they were in the restaurant. Daddy read the signs to them as they waited for the pie to come.

It didn't take long for it to arrive and it didn't take them any time at all to polish it off! Daddy wiped Annie's face and asked her how she managed to get some of the pie on her nose. Annie giggled and licked her lips one more time.

The sound of motorcycles coming down the road turned their attention to the window. It looked like there were fifty motorcycles all turning into the parking lot! Annie was frightened. She didn't know anyone who road a motorcycle and the riders, with their black leather jackets and helmets, looked scary to her.

Their waitress didn't look frightened, though. She looked happy to see them and said, "Looks like the motorcycle group from Germany is here!"

Daddy looked puzzled. "From Germany?"

She replied, "Yes, there are Route 66 fans from all over the world. The group coming in is from Germany. But we get motorcycle groups from all over Europe. They say riding a motorcycle is the best way to travel Route 66. They love America and we love having them at The Midpoint!"

Bobby asked, "But how do they get their motorcycles here? They can't drive them from Germany!"

The motorcycle riders started coming into the Café and the

waitress turned to greet them without answering Bobby's question. They were laughing and talking in a language that the Mouse family didn't understand. Even though Annie couldn't understand them, now that she knew they were Route 66 travelers, they didn't look scary anymore.

Sam said, "See, Mommy, motorcycles aren't so bad."

Mommy just glared at him and he knew he better not say anything more.

Daddy said he thought they should be on their way if they were going to make it to Tucumcari for the night. They smiled and waved at the motorcycle riders on the way out the door. Annie was pleased when they smiled and waved back. She just wished she understood what they were saying!

Once they started down the road again, Bobby asked, "So how DID they get their motorcycles here? No one answered me!"

Daddy answered, "Well, I'm not sure, but they probably flew to Chicago and rented the motorcycles there. We'll have to ask the next time we see another group."

Mommy said, "That sure is something, isn't it? Folks traveling from all over the world to see our beautiful country! Pretty amazing, isn't it? Look at how lucky we are to live here!"

Annie wasn't sure how her brothers and sisters felt, but she knew she felt pretty lucky!

Glenrio was the last town along the route in Texas. Annie looked out the window and saw many boarded up houses and buildings. It made her feel sad. Everyone got very quiet as they drove through yet another town that Daddy called a "ghost town." Sam and Bobby said they had read about ghost towns in their Social Studies classes, but had no idea what they really looked like until seeing them along the route.

"Can we stop and look for real ghosts, Daddy?" Sam asked as they drove by an abandoned gas station.

Bobby shouted, "Look, Annie! Isn't that a ghost in that window over there?"

The triplets started to cry. "We don't want to see any ghosts, Daddy! Can we get back on the highway- quick?!"

Jenny thought it would be fun to find some ghosts. "No, Daddy, let's stop and find that ghost! Maybe he'll talk to us."

Annie pulled her blanket over her head. In a muffled voice, she asked Daddy if he was really going to stop and look for ghosts.

The triplets screamed in unison, "NO, DON"T STOP! PLEASE, DADDY."

Mommy yelled for everyone to settle down. "Stop teasing the little ones this minute!" She reminded them that Daddy would turn the car around and go back home if they did not behave.

Once the children quieted down, Daddy explained that "ghost town" was a term used to describe a town that was left empty after all of the people moved away. "We're not going to be looking for ghosts, but we can look at the old buildings and think about the people who once lived in them."

There was complete silence in the car as they continued through Glenrio.

Chapter Seventeen:
New Mexico: The Land of Enchantment

When they crossed into New Mexico, they discovered that they were still in Glenrio! It was the last town in Texas AND the first town in New Mexico!

Mommy said the travel guide explained that Route 66 changed through the years and they could drive the original, scenic, dirt road option or the newer, paved alignment to San Jon. Daddy chose the original, dirt road option.

Mommy thought maybe Daddy had made a mistake because it seemed like they were driving through a pasture for many miles! They saw many abandoned buildings and cars, and even a building with the words, "Modern Restrooms" written on the side.

The dirt road was so dry that clouds of dust began swirling all around the car. Annie complained that she could hardly see anything through the windows. Daddy agreed the dust was making it hard for him to see where he was driving on the road! He began driving even slower than he had been. "I'm glad most of the route is paved now," he said.

Sally asked, "Is New Mexico in the United States, or are we in Mexico now?"

Jenny rolled her eyes and was about to make a mean comment, but Bobby quickly and gently answered, "This is still the United States, Sally."

Annie didn't want to admit that she had been wondering the same thing.

Daddy said he'd heard that people who lived in New Mexico were often mistaken for being residents of Mexico when traveling to other states. "It's a shame that every adult in the United States doesn't realize that New Mexico is one of the states," he added.

Annie picked up her notebook and began writing numbers one through fifty down one side of the page. "Let's see if we could name all of the states before we stop again."

Her siblings began shouting out the state names faster than she could write. She started out with Pennsylvania, Ohio, Indiana and then wrote down each of the eight Route 66 states. That was as far as she got when they entered Tucumcari.

She put her notebook down as soon as she began to see really cool signs everywhere! Mommy said they'd be staying in Tucumcari for the night so they could see the neon signs all lit up. Daddy drove up and down the main street of town so they could see everything before deciding where they would like to stop.

As it began to get dark, the neon signs started to come on and the whole town was lit up in color. Everyone started to "ooh" and "aw" the same way they did for the Fourth of July fireworks! Annie was excited to be able to take pictures of the neon signs at night.

Annie pointed to the sign for the Motel Safari and said, "Look at the camel!" As Sam read from the guidebook, everyone was surprised to learn that camels had once roamed Tucumcari. They were used to help carry supplies for the surveyors who were trying to map out roadways through the region.

Daddy said, "Maybe we'll stay here tonight."

Mommy said, "Nope. Didn't you see the "no vacancy" sign?"

Annie asked what that meant and Mommy explained there were no more rooms left for the night.

Billy, pointing, said, "Birdy, birdy."

Turning to the direction where he was pointing, they spotted the magnificent neon sign for The Blue Swallow Motel. Daddy drove through the parking lot so they could see the garages he had read about in his guidebook.

Mommy asked, "DO you think we could stay HERE tonight?" But as soon as she said it, the "no vacancy" sign lit up.

Daddy said, "We better look for a room now- if there are any left!"

Daddy pulled into the parking lot of the Historic Route 66 Motel. "I'll check here to see if any rooms are left."

Moments later, Daddy came out with a key. "We got the last room left! There's a conference in town and most of the rooms are booked in Tucumcari. We only got this room because of a last-minute cancellation!"

As they entered the room, Mommy said, "It looks like we got lucky!" She was very pleased with the room. Everything was neat and clean. Annie fell asleep as soon as her head hit the pillow!

They got up bright and early the next morning. Mommy wanted to watch the sun rise. Daddy suggested walking over to the motel's coffee bar, so they could enjoy their breakfast while watching the spectacular colors of the New Mexico sun rise. Even Jenny agreed that it was something special to see!

There was so much to see in Tucumcari that they decided to spend the whole day.

Everyone got excited about the dinosaur museum so Mommy said it should be their first stop. Annie was so excited about seeing dinosaurs that she jumped out of the car and ran to the door, forgetting her camera in the car. Later, she was sorry that she had forgotten it because she wouldn't have any pictures to share with Molly. The whole family enjoyed the museum.

Bobby was the first to notice that Tucumcari also had many murals. He thought he'd like to be an artist someday so he closely examined each one. Mommy thought it was fascinating that they'd seen so many murals in towns across Route 66, yet they were all so different. Daddy said it showed that every community had its own personality.

They all thought Tee Pee Curios looked like it could be a fun stop and it was! Daddy bought all of the children tee shirts with a picture of the shop on it.

Annie wished she could buy one for her friend Molly Mole so they could wear them together when she got home from their trip. She asked Daddy if she could spend a little bit of her souvenir money to buy a shirt for Molly Mole. Daddy thought it was a great idea! Annie couldn't wait to see the look on Molly's face when she gave her the gift she'd picked out for her. Daddy was proud of Annie for always thinking about others.

As they left Tee Pee Curios, Mommy asked Annie if she thought about her own souvenir yet. Annie said she was going to wait until she got to the Grand Canyon to decide.

As Daddy drove down the road, Sally pointed to a large hat on top of a restaurant called La Cita and asked "What's that?"

Mommy explained it was a Mexican hat, called a sombrero. She explained they were designed to protect people from the hot sun. None of them had ever been to a Mexican restaurant before and Daddy asked Mommy what she thought about trying it.

All the kids said, "Say yes, Mommy! We want to see what it's like!"

Mommy agreed and they all enjoyed their first Mexican restaurant experience. Annie loved her taco!

After lunch, their next stop was a shop called Timeless Treasures. Daddy said he'd stay outside with the children while Mommy looked around inside. There were license plates from all over the country outside on the fence. Annie wanted to get her list of license plates she'd seen while on the trip so far and see how many from her list were on the fence. The other kids thought that sounded like fun, too.

When Mommy opened the door to come out, she was followed by a big, friendly dog and Gary, the owner of the shop. The dog dropped a Frisbee down at Annie's feet and Gary said the dog wanted to play. Sam grabbed the Frisbee and threw it before Annie had a chance. The dog went running and was back in no time, again, dropping it at Annie's feet.

Gary told Annie, "I think he wants to play with YOU!"

Annie, who had never thrown a Frisbee before, picked it up and tossed it. It didn't go very far, falling only inches from her feet. The dog looked up at Annie, picked up the Frisbee and dropped it at Sam's feet. They all laughed, even Annie!

When it was time to go, Gary told them to be sure to stop on their way back home, since the shop was going to have some changes. It would be called The Tucumcari Trading Post, but he'd still be there and he hoped to see them again.

Mommy commented, "We've been to several places across the

route that are changing their names or owners."

"Businesses along the route are constantly changing. They either change owners or just change to keep up with the times," Gary replied.

On their way out of town, they found another surprise in front of the Tucumcari Convention Center. Daddy said the Route 66 sculpture looked like it had tail fins from an old car on it.

As they drove through Newkirk and Cuervo Sam teased Annie, "Shall we look for more ghosts?"

Annie remarked that he couldn't fool her again; she knew what a ghost town was now! As she looked at the buildings while Daddy drove slowly through Cuervo, she couldn't believe that even a church and school buildings were left abandoned. They all agreed that the church was their favorite building. Mommy said she couldn't believe that such a pretty building had no Sunday visitors!

They didn't stop again until they arrived in Santa Rosa. Mommy pointed to a sign for The Blue Hole and directed Daddy where to turn so they could explore. Daddy followed the signs to the park. Annie saw some of the bluest water she had ever seen! It almost looked like the blue that Mommy put in the water when they colored Easter eggs!

The sign said that the Blue Hole was 81 feet deep! The people swimming in the water were all wearing special diving suits. They learned that the water temperature was only 64 degrees. They watched the divers for several minutes before going back to the car to discover what else Santa Rosa had to offer.

Daddy grinned when he saw a car high up on top of a pole that announced it was a Route 66 Auto Museum. As Daddy pulled into the parking lot he told Mommy, "This one's for me!"

She laughed and said, "With all the antique shopping you've done for me, I guess you deserve it!"

The stop might have been for Daddy, but they all enjoyed the attraction. There were lots of old cars and antiques to explore. Annie found a sign with the words "Dr. Dave's Snake Oil" on it that made her cringe. Sam said they wouldn't be needing any of THAT and they all agreed!

After they left the museum, Jenny pointed to a sign for the Silver

Moon Restaurant. "Look, Daddy! It says it has Mexican American cooo, caaaa... What's that word?"

"The word is "cuisine" and it's the way the food is cooked, so it means this restaurant has food prepared the same way they make it in Mexico," Daddy answered.

Jenny said she liked the Mexican restaurant in Tucumcari and wondered if it was dinner time yet. Mommy laughed and said, "Not yet, but we could get a snack of chips and salsa."

Daddy said, "Great idea! While we're waiting for the chips to come, we could look at the map and decide where to go next."

As soon as they were seated in the booth, Daddy spread the map across the table. Daddy looked at Mommy and said, "It looks like we have another choice to make. We could take the Santa Fe loop or take a new alignment."

Mommy said she thought they should save the Santa Fe loop for the return trip home. "I think the kids are starting to get eager to get to the Grand Canyon."

Annie overheard and asked if they'd be at the Grand Canyon soon. She was getting excited. The triplets all chimed in with, "Yeah, when will we be there?"

Jenny said it seemed like they'd been driving in the car forever! "Are we EVER going to get there," she asked.

Mommy said it might not be for a few more days, so they just had to be patient! Daddy said they'd have to make some decisions. If they wanted to stop and see everything it would take longer to get there. If they wanted to get there quickly, he could hop on I-40 and they could be there a lot sooner.

He asked, "Should we forget about the rest of Route 66 and get to the Grand Canyon quickly?"

Annie couldn't imagine missing ANY of Route 66. She was the first to answer, "I'll be patient. Don't get on the interstate, Daddy!" The others agreed. Even Jenny.

On their way to Moriarty an animal ran across the road, right in front of the car. Daddy said, "Did you see that moose?" Mommy said, "That wasn't a moose; it was a deer." Sam said, "I never saw a deer that looked like that!" Annie took a picture of it and hoped to be able to identify it when they got home.

After that, the miles rolled by uneventfully. They started to stare out the windows, but on their full bellies, they soon felt drowsy and, one-by-one, all fell asleep.

Mommy told Daddy that she was thankful for the quiet. She knew it wouldn't last long!

A sculpture of running horses welcomed them to Moriarty. Daddy thought the children would want to see it so he started to call their names. "Sam, Bobby, Jenny, Annie..."

Annie jumped awake and rubbed her eyes. "Where are we?" she shouted. "Are we at the Grand Canyon?"

The rest of the kids were now wide-awake and getting excited, when Mommy laughed and said to Daddy, "You had to wake them up, didn't you?"

Sam read the name of the town and Bobby found it on their map. "We're not even to Albuquerque yet!"

As Daddy drove through Moriarty, he passed another Mexican restaurant and commented, "I think we're going to start seeing many more Mexican restaurants in New Mexico." This one had a star high up on the pole above the restaurant. Mommy read from the guidebook that this was called a "rotosphere" and was an example of "Googie-style" architecture that was popular in the 1950s.

The triplets started to chant, "googie, googie, googie." All the children broke into squeals of giggles until Daddy yelled, "ENOUGH!"

Mommy continued reading from the guidebook, then said, "We saw another example of this type of architecture back in Santa Rosa when we saw the restaurant with the balls on top of it."

Annie said she'd have to go through her pictures when they got home so they could find more "Googie-style" examples.

As Daddy continued past Moriarty, Bobby asked if anyone else noticed all of the colorful, rocky, mountains.

Sam said that the mountains back home were tree covered so they looked green this time of year. Annie said she didn't think she'd ever seen rocks this colorful.

Suddenly, Annie shouted, "That car that just passed us had an

Arizona license plate. Are we getting close to Arizona, Daddy?"

All the kids started to get excited, but Daddy said, "I thought you were going to be patient! We're only half way through New Mexico so it will be awhile before we get there."

Annie slid down in her seat, embarrassed. She thought she WAS being patient! But, she had to admit, she was getting very excited!

As they approached Albuquerque, Mommy said it was important that everyone drink some water because she didn't want anyone getting sick. "We're very high up now and I read in the travel guide that some people get something called 'altitude sickness' because the city is so high above sea level."

Annie said, "Let me have a bottle of water. If anyone is going to get sick, I'm sure it will be me!" They all laughed in agreement!

Once in Albuquerque, they drove down Central Avenue. Annie had a difficult time taking pictures because there were so many cool things to photograph, but Daddy couldn't slow down enough for her to get all of the pictures. Annie was disappointed until Daddy pulled into the parking lot of The Dog House. As Annie took a picture of the "wiener dog" on the sign, Daddy said to Mommy, "That's where I am all the time."

Annie was shocked! "I didn't know you came to Albuquerque all the time, Daddy!"

This time, Sam, Bobby AND Jenny all rolled their eyes at Annie and laughed. Annie had no idea why they were laughing at her and she didn't like it!

She soon forgot all about the teasing when Daddy said they should all go inside and get some hot dogs. Mommy said she wanted to try the 66 Diner and Daddy suggested they get milkshakes there after having their hot dogs.

Annie said the inside of the 66 Diner reminded her of the Polk-a-Dot Diner in Illinois. When Mommy asked her why, she pointed to Betty Boop and said, "Isn't that the same girl?"

Daddy said, "I think you're right, Annie. Good memory!"

The children enjoyed sitting at the counter, sipping their milkshakes. Their waitress was very friendly and asked if they'd been to Old Town Albuquerque yet. When Daddy responded that they had not, she said they weren't far and thought they would enjoy it.

Mommy asked Daddy, "Guess where we're stopping next?"

"Oh good! More shopping," Daddy joked.

On the way to Old Town, Bobby read from the travel guide that the buildings they were about to see were adobe. Annie asked what that meant.

Sam said, "I learned all about adobe buildings in my Social Studies class, but I'm not gonna tell you."

Jenny said, "That's 'cause you don't remember!"

"Sam! Jenny! Let Bobby finish," Annie pleaded. Annie was curious to hear what the travel guide said.

Bobby continued reading silently before telling them that it meant that the buildings were made from mud bricks. Annie didn't think she'd ever seen an adobe building before. Mommy said she was pretty sure Cousins Mary and Bob's house in California was adobe so they'd all be staying in one soon enough.

Mommy was relieved that it hadn't taken them long at all to get to Old Town. Daddy easily found a parking spot and in no time at all, they were exploring Old Town.

Annie liked the adobe buildings. Sam said it looked just like the pictures of Mexico in his Social Studies book. Native American artisans were selling their goods on blankets along the street. Annie liked looking at all of the jewelry and was amazed to be able to meet the people who made the pretty items. She noticed that many of the items were made with a pretty blue stone that Mommy called turquoise. Blue was Annie's favorite color and she thought the stones were beautiful.

Sam and Bobby admired the quartz chess sets in one of the shops. Bobby said he wished he knew how to play chess. Secretly, he wished he hadn't bought his drum already; he really liked the carved horses in one of the sets.

Daddy saw how Bobby was admiring it and surprised everyone when he said he was going to buy the set for the family. "I'm pretty sure Cousin Bob knows how to play chess. He could teach us while we're there."

Mommy said, "That's a great idea! Why don't you buy two sets—one for us and one as a gift for Cousin Bob?"

While the chess sets were being wrapped up for them, the clerk asked if they had been to Acoma yet. Mommy asked, "What's that?"

The clerk continued, "The Acoma Pueblo is also called "Sky City" and has been inhabited since 1150 A.D. You can tour the community and learn all about the Southwest Indians. I think your family would enjoy it."

All of the Mouse children excitedly asked at once, "Can we go there, Daddy? Pleeeease?"

Daddy explained that it would take them longer to get to the Grand Canyon if they stopped. Mommy said that maybe they could hop on the interstate for just a little while to make up some time. As much as they hated the idea of getting off of Route 66, they all agreed that they would like to see the "Sky City".

Daddy followed the signs on the interstate that directed him to Old Acoma. After what seemed like a very long drive to the anxious children, Daddy finally entered the parking lot of the Cultural Center.

Inside the Cultural Center, they learned that Acoma is the oldest continuously inhabited community in North America. They discovered this was home to 4800 tribal members and the homes did not have running water or electricity. They were also informed that visitors must follow the laws established by the Tribal Indians while on their land. They could purchase a camera permit, but any photographs they took could only be used for their personal enjoyment.

Suddenly Annie KNEW what she wanted her special souvenir to be! "Daddy, can I have a special camera permit as my special souvenir? I want to be able to remember everything about this place once we are home."

Daddy agreed that getting a camera permit would be a great idea. Daddy added, "But Annie, that's a gift for the whole family to enjoy. I'll buy a permit for my camera and you can take a few pictures with it. Then you can still pick out a special souvenir, just for you." Annie quickly agreed!

After paying for their tour tickets, they joined others who were also waiting for the tour to begin. Before starting the tour, their guide informed them they had to stay with the tour group at all times. No one was to go off and explore on their own. Annie felt her cheeks getting red as the whole family turned to look at her.

Jenny said, "Did you hear that, Annie?"

Annie just stared at the ground, embarrassed. Daddy gave Jenny that look that said she'd better apologize to Annie, so she did.

Once the tour began, they quickly understood why it was called Sky City. Mommy said she felt like they were on top of the world. Daddy said he thought the view was the most incredible he had ever seen! Surprisingly, even Jenny agreed with both of her parents.

After finishing the tour, Sam said he couldn't imagine living without running water and flush toilets. Mommy and Daddy said they could remember a time when their grandparents' homes didn't have indoor plumbing. Annie said she was glad there home did! Everyone laughed.

Even though it was very hot out and they did a lot of walking, no one complained. They were enjoying the incredible view from high on top the mesa and learning all about the Acoma Pueblo.

Once they were back in the car and headed towards the interstate, everyone began talking about the experience they just had. Sam said it was so much better experiencing the Native American land than reading about it in a Social Studies textbook. "Sometimes I find those books boring. This wasn't boring at all!"

Bobby said it sure would make it easier for him to read the textbooks after seeing everything firsthand.

Annie said her favorite stop along the tour was the Franciscan Mission Church and cemetery. Mommy agreed that was her favorite stop, too.

"The whole experience was MY favorite. It may take us a while longer to get to the Grand Canyon, but it was definitely worth the stop," Daddy added.

Their next stop off of the interstate was at the Continental Divide. A covered wagon marked the spot where rainfall drains to the west into the Pacific Ocean and to the east into the Atlantic Ocean. They took a few minutes to explore the hogan, which was beside the wagon. Annie asked what the small building was for and Daddy explained that a hogan is a traditional Navajo dwelling.

They stopped inside the trading post nearby for some snacks before continuing their journey.

A HUGE, colorful pot welcomed them to Gallup. Sam read from the travel guide, "Gallup began as a railroad town." Just then, they heard the train whistle and one came down the tracks, parallel to Route 66. The twins loved watching trains go by so Daddy parked the car in the public parking lot in order for them to have a good view. They clapped their hands and squealed until it was out of sight.

Mommy thought it was a good time for a walk. All of the shops had items made with the beautiful blue stones that Annie liked so much. Annie knew Mommy had already told her what they were called, but she couldn't remember. Mommy reminded her the stones were turquoise.

In one shop, Annie pointed to a beautiful horse reared up on its hind legs. It had turquoise eyes. She thought it was the most beautiful horse she had ever seen. She shouted, "Look at that horse! That's what I'd like for MY special souvenir. Can I get THAT, Daddy?"

Daddy looked at the price tag and his shoulders slumped. He said, "Annie, I'm sorry honey, but I can't get this for you. It's much more expensive than I could afford. It's not a toy; you couldn't touch it or play with it even if I could get it for you. It's also very fragile-it would break into a million pieces if you or any of the other kids knocked it over."

Annie thought her father was disappointed in her for asking for such an expensive souvenir. It made her so sad to think her daddy was disappointed in her that she began to cry. Jenny said, "There she goes again" and rolled her eyes, which only made Annie cry harder.

Daddy took her out of the store. He began to scold her for crying about this. "Look, he said, I told you no and that's that, young lady!"

Annie gulped and said, "I'm sorry, Daddy. I'm not crying because you told me no. I'm crying because I asked for something I shouldn't have. How come I always do stupid things?"

Daddy pulled her close and kissed the top of her head. "Annie, there wasn't anything stupid about asking for the horse. It's very pretty. I could see why you liked it. You don't need to feel ashamed for asking. Now, let's dry those eyes and go back in the store. If you find something else you want and it's not right for you, I'll tell you, but you don't need to cry. Deal?"

Annie nodded. But when she went back into the shop she didn't feel like looking for anything else for herself.

Down the street, at Ray's Trading Company Mommy asked why some of the turquoise stones were a light blue and others were much darker and some had gold lines going through them and others were a solid blue.

Ray took a lot of time explaining to Mommy and Daddy that it depended on where the stones were mined. He showed them a map of the different mines in New Mexico and Arizona and then showed them a stone from each of those mines so they could see the difference. Annie thought they were all beautiful.

Annie saw a tiny beaver with tiny blue stones for its eyes. She pointed and said, "Look, Daddy!"

Ray explained to the children that the beaver was actually a Native American fetish or a "good luck" symbol. He then explained that each animal has a special meaning and told Annie that the beaver was a symbol of a builder. Mommy said, "That's a perfect symbol for you, Annie, since you're always making something!"

Annie looked at Daddy and he knew that look meant that she was really asking if she could get it. He laughed and said, "I think we ALL could use a good luck symbol." He told all of the children to pick out their favorite.

Bobby looked down at the ground and said softly, "I already got my drum, Daddy."

He couldn't believe it when Daddy said it didn't matter; ALL of the children could pick out a special fetish!

Annie asked, "You mean I still get to pick out a special souvenir, even though I'm getting the beaver with the turquoise eyes?!" She thought the good-luck beaver was already working! Mommy and Daddy laughed!

By the time they left Ray's Trading Company they knew they'd made more new friends.

Their final stop of the day was at the El Rancho Motel. The sign out front said it was the "Home of the Movie Stars!" As they walked through the lobby, they all exclaimed, "WOW!" at once.

Mommy said, "This place is beautiful! Look at that fireplace!" Mommy instructed the children to sit down in front of the fireplace while Daddy checked to see if there was a room available. The couches and chairs around the fireplace looked so inviting that no one complained. Annie settled into a space on the couch and wondered if anyone else felt as tiny as she did next to the huge staircase that led to the upstairs rooms.

A few minutes later, Daddy returned with a room key. They began walking through the halls, exploring the motel as they looked for their room. Daddy read names on the doors as they passed by, "Jimmy Stewart, Jackie Cooper, James Cagney, Lee Marvin..."

"Who are they, Daddy?" Jenny asked.

"They're famous old-time movie stars," Daddy answered with excitement in his voice.

Mommy and Daddy sounded really excited as they continued reading the names, but Annie and her brothers and sisters had no idea who those people were. They looked at each other, puzzled, and just shrugged their shoulders.

Daddy could see their confusion and said he'd have to rent some old movies for them to see who some of these actors were.

Finally, Daddy stopped in front of the room that had the name John Wayne on it. "Well, here we are! This is where we're staying for the night."

Annie was confused. She asked, "How could we stay in THIS room? Isn't this John Wayne's room? I don't want to stay with a stranger, even if he IS a movie star!" She explained, "I KNOW that the sign said, 'Home of the movie stars.' Don't the stars LIVE here? I thought there would be rooms with no names on them for people like us, just staying for the night."

Once again, Annie had misunderstood. Once again, Daddy laughed and explained that it meant that when the stars were making movies a long time ago they stayed here. They didn't live here, but the motel tried to make them feel at home. He wasn't even sure if any of the stars whose names were on the doors were still alive.

Once they were settled in the room, Daddy learned even more about Gallup and the famous motel as he read from the brochure left on the dresser. Gallup had begun as a railroad town. It was chosen to make movies because the trains could bring the stars into the area and the desert made a perfect backdrop for the Western films that were popular during that time. The motel was built in 1937 and was a nice place for the actors and actresses to stay. "Those pictures we saw in the lobby were many of the movie stars who stayed in the motel," Daddy finished.

"Let's go explore the pictures and the rest of the names on the doors, Daddy," Annie said.

The rest of the kids chimed in, "Yeah, Daddy, let's go!"

Daddy looked over at Mommy and she agreed that it would be fun to explore.

As they walked down the halls, Annie was hoping she would know who some of the stars were, but she didn't recognize any of them. She was starting to get bored until Mommy read a door with the name, "Lucille Ball" on it. Annie and Jenny both got excited. Annie said, "We know HER from the I Love Lucy show!" They both loved that television show.

Soon, their exploring took them down a hall into the restaurant. Daddy said he was getting hungry and they all agreed it was a perfect time to have dinner. Afterwards, Mommy said, "Let's get to bed early tonight. Tomorrow we'll be in Arizona."

The kids shouted, "Arizona! THE GRAND CANYON! Will we be seeing the Grand Canyon tomorrow?!"

Daddy said, "It's still a few hundred miles before we get to the Grand Canyon. There's still so much we want to explore, so it will probably be a few more days, but we're almost there!"

Annie was so excited about getting to Arizona; she couldn't fall asleep thinking about it.

Chapter Eighteen:
Arizona

The next morning Mommy and Daddy wanted to get an early start but they had a hard time waking up the children. Sam said, "I was so excited about getting to Arizona, I lay awake all night thinking about it. I must have just fallen asleep!"

Bobby said, "Same with me. Now I'm really tired!" Annie and Jenny both added, "Same here!"

But Annie was eager to continue the trip and ran for the bathroom to get ready. Jenny pushed Annie aside and said, "Hey! I'm older, I get to go into the bathroom first!"

Mommy yelled, "I get to go to the bathroom first and then you'll all take your turn when I tell you. And no dawdling!"

Daddy told the kids to pack their bags while they waited for their turn. He gave them that look that said they'd better listen! A half an hour later, everyone was ready to go.

As they piled into the car, Daddy said it wouldn't be long before they would see the "Welcome to Arizona" sign.

Annie said she wanted to be the first to see the sign for Arizona. But as soon as the car started moving Annie felt her eyelids getting heavy. She watched as each of her siblings fell asleep, but she was determined to see the sign welcoming them to Arizona, so she kept trying to force her eyes to stay open. She listened as the tires thump, thumped on the roadway and before long, even she was asleep.

By the time they reached the sign that said, "Welcome to Arizona," only Daddy was awake to see it.

Daddy pulled the car into the parking lot of the Arizona Welcome Center. When he turned the car off, Annie jumped awake and shouted, "Where ARE we? Did I miss the sign? DAAAAADDY, why didn't you wake me up?" The rest of the Mouse children groggily wiped their eyes and began to wake up.

Daddy said, "Look, you can still see the "Welcome to Arizona" sign from here! That's why I pulled over, so you wouldn't miss it." All the children cheered when they saw the sign!

Mommy said they should go inside to see what kinds of brochures they had. Annie liked looking at the brochures from visitors centers. Daddy said pretty soon they wouldn't be able to fit the kids in the car with all the brochures they were picking up!

While Mommy and Daddy signed the visitors' book, Annie found a brochure for the Grand Canyon Railway. She started jumping up and down, shouting, "Mommy, Daddy! Look what I found! Can we ride the train to the Grand Canyon?"

Jenny grabbed for Annie's brochure saying, "Where'd you find that? I want it!"

Annie held onto it tighter, "It's mine. I saw it first. Get your own," she cried to Jenny.

Then ALL the kids wanted their own brochure. Mommy and Daddy were embarrassed with the noise their children were making. Everyone began to stare.

Daddy quickly got their attention when he asked in a stern voice, "Shall we turn around and go back to Pennsylvania?"

In an instant they all quieted down. Daddy continued, "Everyone back in the car, NOW!"

Mommy and Daddy apologized to the staff. A kind lady gave Mommy a stack of brochures and some coloring books she thought would keep the children occupied. Mommy was very grateful.

Back in the car, Mommy told the children that their behavior in the visitor's center had been unacceptable and wouldn't be tolerated.

Annie was the first to apologize. "Sorry, Mommy. I just got so excited when I saw that brochure I forgot to mind my manners."

The others quickly chimed in with their own apologies. No one wanted to go back to Pennsylvania now that they were THIS close to the Grand Canyon!

With everyone calmed down, Mommy handed each of the children a brochure and coloring book.

Down the street from the visitor's center, there were many Indian Trading Posts selling Native American blankets, pottery and jewelry. Daddy told Mommy they wouldn't be able to stop at them all. "We'll NEVER make it to the Grand Canyon if we do." Mommy agreed with Daddy but admitted that it was hard to decide which stops to make.

Daddy said he learned at the Welcome Center that he would have no choice but to get on the interstate every now and again, since there were several places where Route 66 was cut off or the road wasn't very good. Daddy decided they would take the interstate rather than take a chance on roads that might not be passable.

When they began seeing dinosaurs and teepees along the roadside, all the kids begged Daddy to get off the interstate so they could check them out. Daddy exited at Adamana Road and pulled into Stewart's Rock Shop parking lot.

The boys thought the dinosaur that looked like it was eating a woman was cool, but the girls squealed, "eeewww!" Daddy laughed and said, "The dinosaurs aren't real. They can't hurt you."

Mommy pointed to the fence and warned them not to get too close. "The dinosaurs are fake, but those are real ostriches and might bite!"

While the children explored outside with Mommy, Daddy went inside and bought a pouch of colorful rocks. Before getting back in the car, he showed them to the children and explained they were actually petrified wood, not rocks. "When we get to the motel tonight, I'll pour them out so you could each choose one," Daddy said.

Across the road, at The Painted Desert Indian Center, they saw more beautiful turquoise jewelry and more petrified wood. There were many things that Mommy and Daddy said were "fragile" so they knew they needed to be very careful. The children were all on their best behavior.

Mommy pointed to a row of vases on a shelf, "Look, Annie, there's more of that pottery that looks like the horse you liked."

The shop owner told them it was called horse hair pottery. She explained it was an American Indian art form using actual horse hair to create the interesting designs. They noticed that each piece was very different. Annie thought they were all beautiful.

Mommy suggested that Annie and Jenny help pick out a vase to take to Cousin Mary since they did not yet have a gift for her. Annie was pleased when Mommy said the one she picked out was perfect! Annie would be able to tell Mommy's relatives that she was the one who had chosen the special gift!

When Mommy was done paying for the vase, the owner wrapped it carefully, and then surprised Mommy by giving her a piece of colorful, petrified wood to take with them as a special souvenir. Mommy said she would always treasure it!

Their next stop was in Holbrook. They saw a sign that said "Home of the HASHKNIFE Pony Express." Sam said he'd learned in his Social Studies class that mail used to be delivered by men riding horses.

Bobby, who had been reading the travel guide, said excitedly, "Guess what?! It says here that Pony Express riders still deliver the mail from Holbrook to Scottsdale once a year as a special celebration. You could mail yourself a letter and have it postmarked with The Pony Express! Let's do that when we get back home!" Annie, Jenny and Sam all agreed they would like to mail letters through the Pony Express[12].

Over a yummy lunch at Joe & Aggies Café, Mommy and Daddy discussed whether they should go to the Petrified Forest National Park. Their waitress told them it was definitely worthwhile. The children were eager to get to the Grand Canyon, but they were so close to the Petrified Forest from the Café parking lot they could see the signs pointing them to the National Park. It was unanimous; how COULD they pass it up?!

---

12   Scan the code for instructions on mailing a letter via Pony Express or visit http://tinyurl.com/lz9u4rf.

The waitress asked them if they had stopped at the Navajo County Museum yet. Daddy said they hadn't and asked her where it was. She pointed out the window, "You're so close, you could walk there. It's worth a stop and won't take you long to see it."

Mommy thought a short walk after such a big lunch seemed like a good idea.

The Navajo County Museum was inside what used to be the Courthouse Building, surrounded by an iron fence. Daddy reading the sign posted on the door said, "Too bad we won't be here tonight when there will be an Indian dance in the courtyard."

Even though it was a disappointment to miss seeing a tribal dance, there were many interesting things to see inside. The jail was the most interesting to Annie and her brothers and sisters. Sam commented, "At least this one is inside. Not like all those others we saw."

After leaving the museum, on their way to the National Park, the triplets shouted, pointing to another rock shop, "Look, Daddy! More dinosaurs!"

Daddy stopped for the red light right before the shop, then drove past the Rock Shop with the dinosaur sculptures out front when the light turned green. Mommy thought it was for the best, since they wanted to get to the park. Annie was happy that Daddy had gotten a red light since she was able to take some great pictures while they were stopped.

As Daddy followed the signs to the Petrified Forest National Park, the triplets kept asking, "Are we there yet?" It seemed to be taking a very long time to get there. After the fifth time they asked,

Daddy warned them not to ask again!

When they finally saw the sign for the park all the kids shouted at once, "There it is!"

At the entrance they were greeted by a park ranger who explained that it was against the law to remove anything from a National Park. He warned, "It might look tempting to pick a flower, or take a rock with you, but you will have to pay a fine if you do!"

Mommy and Daddy asked if all of the children heard that. Annie asked if she was allowed to take pictures. The ranger laughed and said, "Yes, that is the ONLY thing you are allowed to take from the park!" Annie was relieved.

Daddy looked at Mommy and said, "I think we could enjoy looking out the window while I drive through the park. That way we won't have to worry about anyone picking up anything they shouldn't." Mommy nodded in agreement.

As Daddy drove slowly through the park, Annie kept snapping pictures; each mountain of stone was more colorful than the last. Every time they saw another colorful rock formation, Annie and her brothers and sisters would let out a gasp and squeal with delight.

Mommy heard so many "oohs and ahs" that she laughed and said it sounded like the children were watching the Fourth of July fireworks!

Jenny said, "I had no idea rocks could be THIS colorful!" For once, Annie had to agree with her sister.

Daddy decided to do a complete loop of the park and go out the same way they went in so they could continue on Route 66 where they left off.

Once out of the park, they continued through Holbrook. They even saw wigwams that you could stay in for the night!

Annie asked, "Daddy, could we stay in one of these tonight?"

The rest of the kids chimed in with, "Yeah, Daddy, can we, can we?" Everyone thought it would be a great idea to stay there, but Daddy pointed to the "No Vacancy" sign and by now they all knew what that meant.

A big, disappointed sigh filled the air. Daddy pulled into the parking lot and suggested, "I can drive through the parking lot so we can look at the wigwams for a few minutes."

Sam yelled, "Dad, look at those cars," as he pointed to the old cars parked around the wigwams.

Daddy told Annie to be sure to take pictures of all of the old cars for him. "I'd like to share your pictures with Cousin Bob when we get to California, Annie."

Annie didn't really understand why Daddy and Sam got so excited about old cars, but she liked being able to do something special for Daddy. She took lots of photos for him.

As they drove out of the parking lot, Mommy said, "Maybe there will be a vacancy on our way home."

As Daddy continued driving, he pointed to a huge billboard with the picture of a rabbit that announced, "HERE IT IS." They all wondered what "IT" was so they just had to stop and find out!

"It" turned out to be The Jack Rabbit Trading Post. Mommy bought them a treat of what looked like tiny rocks from the Painted Desert but they were yummy candies! Before they got back in the car, they all took turns sitting on the huge jack rabbit outside. Annie asked Sam to take a picture of her with Mommy and Daddy in front of it.

Once in the car, Bobby continued reading from the travel guide and announced that Winslow wasn't too far away.

Suddenly, the sky turned brown and the wind rocked the car back and forth. Daddy gripped the steering wheel tightly and Mommy looked scared. When Daddy could no longer see where he was going, he eased the car to the side of the road. "Let's sit here until this dust storm dies down." Mommy agreed. Sam said it looked just like when they had blizzards in Pennsylvania, but this one was brown.

When the worst of the storm died down, Daddy continued driving until they got to Winslow. When he saw the corner with a statue of a man holding a guitar beside a street sign with the words, "STANDIN ON THE CORNER," he parked the car[13].

---

13   Standin' on the Corner is from the song 'Take it Easy' sung by The Eagles and written by Jackson Browne and Glenn Frey. Scan the code for more information on the Standin' on the Corner Park in Winslow or visit http://tinyurl.com/khkllj6.

Mommy and Daddy started to sing, "Standin' on the corner in Winslow, Arizona..." The children just stared at them. Daddy and Mommy looked at each other and laughed.

Suddenly, Bobby said, "Hey, listen! Do you hear that song playing? That's what Mommy and Daddy are singing! I think it's coming from that store on the corner!"

Daddy explained that it was one of his and Mommy's favorite songs when they were teenagers. Mommy said, "I never knew back then that Winslow, Arizona was a real place!"

Annie handed her camera to Daddy and asked, "Will you take my picture by the statue?"

Just as Daddy snapped her picture, a big gust of wind kicked up and Annie grabbed on to the statue. She joked, "I think they should be singing 'Blowin' off a corner in Winslow, Arizona!" Everyone laughed.

Jenny pointed to the street and asked, "Did anyone notice the Route 66 shield in the middle of the road?"

"Wow! That has to be the biggest Route 66 shield we've seen yet!" Annie exclaimed.

The triplets started to run towards the shield. As Sally began to step into the street, she said, "Let's go walk on it!" Her sisters were running right behind her.

Mommy and Daddy yelled, "NO! STOP! Freeze," as they each grabbed one of the girls. A car flew past them and Sally realized what she had almost done. She began to cry. Daddy said sternly, "It's time to get back in the car." No one argued.

Not too far down the road stood a beautiful building with a sign that said, "La Posada." Bobby read from the guidebook that it was a hotel that cost one million dollars to build in 1929 and had been designed by a woman.

Mommy said she thought it looked like the perfect place to stay for the night. Daddy agreed, saying he was ready to stop for the night since he felt a little shaken up with Sally almost getting hit by the car.

Annie was glad she wasn't the one who caused everyone to get upset for a change. But she was REALLY glad her sister didn't run out into the street and get hit by a car.

As they got out of the car, Sam pointed across the street to another building. He asked, "Isn't that one of those Valentine Diners over there?"

Everyone looked towards the small building that hadn't been painted in a long time. It looked abandoned.

Bobby replied softly, "I guess that's what they look like when they aren't being used anymore."

Annie imagined what it must have looked like when it was still a diner and people ate there. She thought it looked lonely across the street from this beautiful hotel.

As they walked towards the entrance of the hotel, Daddy said, "I sure do hope someone buys it and makes it look like the one we saw next to the museum in Oklahoma. It sure would be nice to see it open for business, too. It would be a shame to see it sit like that with no one ever eating in it again."

As they walked through the lobby, Mommy admired the antiques and statues. There were paintings and sculptures everywhere.

Mommy reminded the children not to touch anything! She decided to take all of the children out into the garden while Daddy took care of getting a room.

When Daddy came back with their room key, he told them that only well-behaved children were allowed to stay at the hotel. "If anyone misbehaves, we'll be asked to leave." They ALL knew what THAT meant!

On the way to their room, they walked around the back of the building and discovered the railroad tracks. Daddy said he learned that the Santa Fe Railroad built the hotel and people used to ride the train right to the hotel. He also found out that the current owners were artists and they bought the hotel when they learned it was going to be torn down. It hadn't been used as a hotel in a long time and had been neglected, just like some of the other buildings they had seen along the way. But the people who bought it thought it was too special to be destroyed. They put a lot of work into it so it could be reopened.

Annie couldn't imagine this beautiful hotel being torn down! She suddenly had a thought! "Daddy, are they going to fix up the Valentine Diner, too?"

Daddy said he hadn't thought to ask them, but he learned they were fixing up another hotel in California. "We'll be going right past in on the way to Cousin Mary and Bob's house," he added.

As they made their way to their room, they stopped to look at many of the paintings and sculptures that decorated the halls. Daddy said that many of them were created by the hotel's owners. Mommy wanted to spend more time wandering through the hotel, looking at the art work without worrying about the children accidentally breaking something. Daddy took the children to the room, read them a bedtime story and put them to bed. They were exhausted from their long day.

The next morning, they enjoyed their breakfast out in the garden. Mommy said having breakfast in this garden made her feel like the Queen of England and she wouldn't mind living here.

Annie thought it was beautiful, but she couldn't imagine never going back to their home on the farm! She was enjoying this adventure, but she was already starting to miss her home and her friend, Molly Mole.

Mommy interrupted Annie's thoughts of home by saying, "Okay, everyone, off to the restrooms before we leave!"

Jenny whined, "Why do I have to keep going to the bathroom when I don't HAVE to go?"

Daddy answered sternly, "If you don't go now, I won't stop the car in a few minutes when you tell me you have to go!"

All the kids groaned, but did as they were told before checking out of the hotel and continuing their trip.

Daddy was the first to see the dome-shaped building on the side of the road. They all wanted to find out what it was. As Daddy pulled into the parking lot, they all read the words painted on the side of the building: "World's Longest Map of U.S. Route 66." They had fun pointing to all of the places they had already visited. This was the Meteor City Trading Post. Annie was disappointed that it wasn't open. Daddy said he couldn't tell if it wasn't open for the day yet, or was permanently closed. "We'll have to check it out on our way back home and see[14]."

---

14   The Meteor City Trading Post closed in December of 2012 and, at the time of this book's publication was for sale. Sadly, the map has been slowly fading.

Back on the road, they began to see signs for The Meteor Crater. Mommy asked Daddy if he thought they should stop there. In answer, Daddy turned off the interstate and followed the signs. Everyone laughed when they saw a picture of a cow on a crossing sign!

Mommy said, "That sign looks just like the 'deer crossing' signs we have in Pennsylvania!"

They all laughed when Daddy answered, "At least the cows won't try to jump over the car!"

After parking the car, the whole family got excited as they walked past an Apollo space test capsule before entering the Visitor's Center. They all knew exactly what it was. Annie squealed, "Look! It's just like the one in front of the DQ in Franklin[15]!"

Once inside, Mommy said, "I thought we were just going to look at a hole in the ground and be on our way. This looks like we could be exploring here all day!"

Daddy said, "One thing's certain. We won't be seeing the Grand Canyon today."

Their tour began with a short movie, where they learned all about meteorites. After the movie the tour guide gave them a choice. He said they could go outside or view the crater from the indoor viewing area, which is air-conditioned. "If joining me for the outdoor tour," he warned, "you must keep the children away from the rim since there aren't any guard rails and it's a LONG way down!" He added, "570 feet to be exact."

That was enough information to make Mommy decide to stay inside with the smaller children while Daddy went with the older ones to the rim. Annie could already feel her knees start to shake so she held Daddy's hand a lot tighter!

Outside, the guide informed the group that a fiery meteorite crashed down and created the huge crater in the earth about 50,000 years ago.

Sam said, "I hope there weren't any cows standing around here then!" Annie shuddered at that thought and squeezed Daddy's hand

---

15   A similar Apollo space test capsule sits in front of the Franklin, PA Dairy Queen. Scan the code for more information about both the Apollo test capsule and the Meteor Crater or visit http://tinyurl.com/kdppjbb.

even tighter!

After the tour was over, they joined Mommy and the other children in the gift shop. Annie was tempted by many items, but still was not ready to buy her special souvenir.

Sam picked up their travel guide the moment they got back in the car. Daddy wasn't even back to the interstate when Sam yelled to him, "Daddy, you HAVE to stop at "Two Guns."

"We aren't ever going to get to the Grand Canyon at this rate," Daddy replied.

"This won't take long, Daddy. It's another ghost town. It looks like we could see what's there right from the car," Sam reassured him. Sam continued reading from the guidebook as Daddy drove on. He told them that this was Canyon Diablo. There had been several roadside attractions, including a zoo, on this spot over the years but only ruins remained now.

Daddy pulled off of the interstate and started driving down a dirt road. They saw the words, "Mountain Lions" on the side of what was left of one building. Bobby saw a cowboy painted on the side of another building and said, "This looks like it was a fun place for kids when it was open!"

Daddy continued slowly down the dirt road as far as he could, before turning around and getting back on the interstate.

Not far down the road was a sign for Twin Arrows. Daddy asked, "What's the travel guide say about Twin Arrows, Sam?"

Sam replied, "The picture in the guidebook looks cool. It's two big arrows sticking out of the ground. It's just another quick stop, Daddy!"

Everyone begged Daddy to stop so they could see. Daddy laughed and eased the car off of the interstate. He drove through the loop slowly so Annie could take her pictures and everyone could see the remains of the trading post. Everyone agreed that the two arrows sticking straight out of the ground were cool! Annie wondered how they stayed in the ground. Mommy wondered why the trading post wasn't open any longer. "With this heat, you'd think they'd sell a lot of cold drinks to the travelers stopping to see the arrows," she commented.

That made everyone think about how thirsty they were. Daddy

said they would soon be in Flagstaff and he had picked out a great place to stop for lunch, Miz Zip's.

Daddy was glad when he was able to get off of the interstate and continue on Route 66. They all enjoyed the scenery and the slower pace of the traffic so much more than the interstate travel.

As they approached Flagstaff they couldn't believe how green everything suddenly got again. Annie shouted, "Look at all of the Christmas trees. It looks like we're back in Pennsylvania!" It seemed so odd to see all of this green after they had been driving through the desert areas for so long.

As they entered the business district, Daddy told them to watch for the sign for Miz Zip's. Annie saw a really cool sign in the shape of a guitar, so she asked Daddy if he would stop so she could get a picture. Sam and Bobby read the sign at the same time, "The Museum Club."

Mommy said, "I wonder what kind of museum it is. Should we go in?"

Sam read from the guidebook that it was a great place to stop "for night life."

Mommy laughed. "Well, I guess that's not the kind of museum we want to explore!"

Annie guessed they weren't going inside because it was still day time. But she was happy with the pictures she took of the building and sign.

A few minutes later, Mommy told Daddy to slow down. Pointing, she said, "There's Miz Zip's."

Once seated, the twins, who had been so good throughout most of the trip, started to squirm and fuss. Buster knocked over a glass of water and it went splashing across the table and onto the floor.

Daddy quickly grabbed napkins to start mopping up the mess, while Mommy scooped up Buster. Annie sat there, holding her breath. She didn't want to mention that most of the water was in her lap and now it looked like she had peed her pants! They were so close to the Grand Canyon; she didn't want Daddy to turn around and go home now!

Their server heard the commotion and quickly came over, ready to clean up the mess. "Here, let me get that. That's what I'm here for!"

Embarrassed, Mommy apologized and told her they'd been traveling for a long time.

The friendly server reassured them that accidents happen all the time and it was no problem. She asked, "Where are you going?"

At once, the triplets shouted, "THE GRAND CANYON!"

Mommy added that they were from Pennsylvania and had been traveling Route 66 on their way to California. They were all excited about stopping at the Grand Canyon.

The waitress asked them if they knew they could take a train from Williams to the Grand Canyon. "If I were you, I'd take the train. The kids would really like the ride and then you don't need to worry about traffic and parking at the Grand Canyon," she advised.

Sarah, Sandy, and Sally all said at once, "A TRAIN ride! Could we, Daddy, PLEASE?"

Annie remained silent. She didn't want to mention that the brochure that had gotten them all in trouble at the Arizona Welcome Center was the one for the Grand Canyon Railway. She had forgotten to share it with her parents after they had all been sent back to the car.

"Stop at the Visitor's Center downtown. It's only a few miles down the street. You'll want to see Flagstaff's downtown area and you can get the Grand Canyon information there, too," she informed them.

Mommy was thankful that their waitress was so pleasant, even though the children had made such a big mess. Daddy was also thankful for her helpful information. He made sure to leave her a nice big tip when they were done with their juicy burgers!

When they got up to leave, everyone could see Annie's wet pants. Jenny pointed and laughed, "Look everyone, Annie peed her pants!"

Annie protested, shaking her head, "No! It's the water that Buster spilled!"

Mommy asked, "Annie, did you sit there this whole time in those wet pants? Why didn't you tell us?"

One look from Daddy, and the others knew they better not tease!

Annie confessed that she didn't want to cause any more trouble. "I didn't want Daddy to get mad and head for home instead of the Grand Canyon," she confessed. Jenny, once again, rolled her eyes at Annie.

"Come on, Annie, let's get you into a dry pair of shorts." Mommy directed Annie back to the restroom for a quick change while Daddy supervised getting the other children back in the car.

With Annie nice and dry again they were finally headed to downtown Flagstaff.

Only a few minutes later, Daddy was parking the car beside the Visitor's Center in the Santa Fe passenger train depot. Inside, Daddy and Mommy got all of the information they needed for The Grand Canyon Railway. The nice lady at the information counter advised Daddy to follow old Route 66 into Williams.

Mommy picked up many more brochures for all of the other things that they could see in Flagstaff. Excitedly, she said, "Look! We could see the Riordan Mansion, The Lowell Observatory, the..."

Daddy interrupted, "We'll consider those for the trip back home. I think now that we're this close, everyone is anxious to get to Williams, now."

Laughing, Mommy agreed. She slid the brochures into her bag. Before leaving the depot, they stopped to watch a train go by. They had never stood this close to one before! The twins squealed with excitement, clapping their hands. Their excitement at watching a train go by made everyone else laugh, too.

On the drive to Williams, Mommy read the brochure to Daddy so they could decide which tour package they would like to buy when they got to the ticket office. Daddy said, "We'll stay at the hotel tonight and take the morning train, and the guided tour bus at the Grand Canyon." Mommy liked that plan.

An short time later, Daddy was parking the car near the Grand Canyon Railway Depot! Everyone cheered! Daddy was concerned when he saw all of the traffic. It hadn't occurred to him that the hotel and railway might be all booked up. He hoped they would be able to get a room and train tickets.

Mommy waited in the car with the children while Daddy went inside. She pointed to the nearby hotel and explained they would be staying there and riding the train in the morning.

"The morning?! Not tonight?" Sam, Bobby, Jenny and Annie all expressed their disappointment at once.

Mommy laughed and said, "We've waited this long to get here. One more night will go quickly. Don't you want to spend the whole day at the Grand Canyon?"

Annie sighed. It was so hard being patient! But, she had to agree with Mommy- a WHOLE day at the Grand Canyon was better than just one night!

A few minutes later, a smiling Daddy came back and instructed everyone to get out of the car. "Let's take our bags to our room before we explore Williams." To Mommy he whispered, "We're lucky. It's a good thing we got here when we did. I got the last room and the last tickets for the train ride."

The children eagerly jumped out of the car, each grabbing their own bag, and followed Daddy. Annie couldn't wait to see what their next adventure would be!

While Mommy was "freshening up" in their room, Sam read from their travel guide, "Williams is the 'Gateway to the Grand Canyon' and was the last town on Route 66 to be bypassed by the interstate. You will enjoy a true Wild West experience here."

Bobby shouted, "A Wild West experience! Let's go!"

Mommy came out of the bathroom. "What's all the yelling I hear out here?"

"The children are ready for a Wild West experience," Daddy answered.

"Well then, let's go!" Mommy replied.

With the twins in the stroller, they left the room to begin their walking tour of Williams Route 66. The six blocks were filled with shops and restaurants. Bobby and Sam enjoyed looking at the cowboy hats and boots, but they still didn't understand how this was a "Wild West experience."

Suddenly, they heard a commotion in the street behind them. They saw the cowboys coming towards each other. Sam and Bobby were both excited; THIS was what they had been waiting for!

Annie was frightened. "Are they going to shoot each other,

Daddy?"

Daddy took her hand and reassured her it was just a "street show" and these were actors.

Daddy found a good spot on the sidewalk for them to watch. The babies started to cry. It was too noisy for them, so Mommy went into a shop behind them. "I'll be able to watch from the window," she told Daddy.

"So THIS is a Wild West show," Annie thought while she watched the cowboys have a shoot-out. Bobby and Sam were excited. Jenny was trying not to look interested, but Annie could tell she was as excited as her brothers. Annie's favorite part was when the sheriff came and stopped the fight.

After the show was over, Mommy came back outside and said they should get some dinner and get to sleep early. "We need to be on the train early," she reminded them.

Even though she was excited about the Grand Canyon train ride in the morning, Annie fell asleep as soon as they said good night. It had been a long, exciting day!

Chapter Nineteen:

The Grand Canyon-FINALLY!

The alarm went off early the next morning. Annie rubbed the sleep out of her eyes and, for a few seconds, wondered where she was. Then it hit her! Today was the day they were finally going to the Grand Canyon! "Come on everyone! Get up! We don't want to miss our train ride," she shouted.

Her yelling made the babies start to cry. Jenny jumped up and said, "Now look what you did! You made them cry!"

Annie couldn't help it. She was so excited; she didn't want to miss their train ride.

Daddy came over and wondered what all the commotion was about. "Settle down, Annie. I'll make sure everyone is ready on time."

"Sorry, Daddy," she muttered, looking down at the floor. She didn't understand why everyone else wasn't as excited as she was.

It seemed like it was taking forever for her family to get ready! But finally, with everyone ready, they were on the way to the train depot. She had never been on a train before!

As they waited to board the train, they were treated to another

Wild West show. This time, Annie wasn't frightened and even giggled while watching the cowboys. One was even playing a guitar!

Once on the train, Daddy said he was looking forward to being able to enjoy the scenery without worrying about driving through traffic. "I'm looking forward to just sitting back and relaxing," he told Mommy. Mommy reminded him there wouldn't be any relaxing until all of the children were settled!

As the train began moving, a voice came through the speakers giving them information about the train and the land. Annie learned that the train had been taking people to the Grand Canyon since 1901. "Wow! That was a LONG time ago," she gasped. She was even more surprised when a few cowboys started playing their guitars and banjos and singing to them!

Bobby pointed out the window, "Look! There are people riding horses next to the train! It looks like they're trying to stop the train!"

Everyone wondered what was going on. Daddy said, "So much for relaxing! It looks like the train is about to get some visitors!"

Suddenly, Jenny pointed at somebody coming down the aisle, "I wonder why he's wearing a hankie across his face," she said. Annie started to giggle, ready for another show.

Then, she wasn't so sure it was a show! Maybe this man really was going to rob the train! Annie didn't want to admit it, but even if it was a show, she was a little afraid. She buried her head into Daddy's arm and told him to let her know when it was safe to look again!

Daddy reassured her it was all part of a "reenactment," and she didn't need to be afraid. But if they had been on this train in 1901, it wouldn't have been a show and it wouldn't have been fun. Annie was glad that she was on the train NOW and not in 1901! She decided to stay snuggled up against Daddy anyway.

Jenny, who was sitting across from Annie, whispered to her, "You're such a baby!" But Annie thought Jenny looked scared, too.

Bobby and Sam weren't afraid of the "robbers." They were having fun! By the time the train reached the Grand Canyon, they were disappointed that the ride was over and they had to get off!

When they got off of the train they were at the South Rim of the Grand Canyon. The conductor had told them it was the most popular area for tourists to visit. Annie said excitedly, "I can't believe we're HERE!" Jenny added, "FINALLY!" The triplets began jumping up and down and clapping. Mommy told everyone to calm down!

Daddy ordered everyone to follow him to the bus stop. "Since we're only going to spend the day, we're going to take a guided bus tour. That way we'll be able to see and learn a lot more than if we were walking through the park."

Annie could hardly control her excitement as they boarded the tour bus! She had her camera ready.

As the bus began rolling out of the parking lot, their tour guide told them the Grand Canyon is 277 miles long and up to 18 miles wide in some spots. She thought the Meteor Crater was big, but now it seemed tiny in comparison. They were able to see all of the Meteor Crater at once, but Daddy said the only way you could see the Grand Canyon all at once would be if you were up in a plane!

Annie was glad the bus stopped to let them out at several locations. At one stop, they were able to see the Colorado River flowing at the bottom of the canyon. Sam said he thought the Colorado River was bigger than that. "That's just a tiny stream," he exclaimed.

Their guide told them it only looked that small because it was a mile down! "You could take a burro ride to the bottom, or take one of the walking trails down, if you'd like," he added. He pointed off in a distance to what looked like a glass walkway. "Over there, that's the Grand Canyon Skywalk. It's a glass bridge that is 4000 feet over the canyon!"

Annie could feel her knees start to shake just thinking about it!

"Will we be going over the Skywalk?" Mommy asked.

"If you wanted to do that, you would have to go on your own. The Skywalk is on the Hualapai Indian territory and they have their own tours."

"Can we do that?" Sam asked. He thought it would be fun to walk across a glass walkway.

Daddy said, "We'll see." But they all knew when Daddy said, "We'll see" that it usually meant "no."

Bobby said, "I think it would be fun to ride the burros down to the bottom. Could we do that?"

"NO!" Mommy and Daddy both answered at the same time causing everyone to giggle.

Jenny asked Bobby, "Are you crazy? Did you miss the part of the tour guide's presentation that said there were mountain lions and fox throughout the canyon?"

The tour guide interrupted the discussion to say they had to be back on the bus in 15 minutes, so if they took the burro ride down, they'd miss the rest of the tour and the train back to Williams.

Daddy said, "Well, that settles it. We have to be back on the train to return to Williams."

Annie was relieved! As much as she'd like to get a picture of a mountain lion, she wasn't sure she wanted to be that close to one! She had been taking a lot of pictures, but she didn't think any of them looked as spectacular as actually seeing the Grand Canyon in person. She even asked Daddy to take some for her, hoping he could get more of the Grand Canyon than she could, but none of them looked as amazing to her as the Grand Canyon looked. The pictures looked tiny and the Grand Canyon was HUGE! No matter where Annie stood, she felt tinier than she had ever felt before.

The bus made several more stops. They learned that the Grand Canyon was open for visitors all year but sometimes the roads were closed because there was too much snow. "Once, back in 1949, the temperature was -16° F," he said.

"Wow! It rarely gets THAT cold in Pennsylvania," Daddy exclaimed.

Annie was glad that it wasn't that cold now. It made her shiver just hearing about the cold!

Their tour was over all too quickly and it was time to head back to the train station before they knew it. Their guide let them know they had some time to spend in the gift shop before boarding the train.

There, in the gift shop, Annie finally found the perfect souvenir! It was a book about the National Parks with amazing pictures that must have been taken from an airplane! There were pictures from not only the Grand Canyon, but also the Painted Desert and Petrified Forests. She could never take pictures like the ones in this book. Annie showed Daddy the book and shyly asked if it could be her special souvenir. She could not believe her good luck when Daddy agreed! She would treasure this book forever.

Annie held onto her package tightly as they boarded the train. They'd had a long, exciting day and this book would help her remember it even after they were back home. She couldn't wait to share all of it with her best friend!

They all talked excitedly about their day as the train chugged back to Williams. Annie snuggled up against Daddy and thanked him for taking them to the Grand Canyon. Everyone agreed that it was a great adventure, even Jenny.

Daddy asked, "Did we see enough of the Grand Canyon? Should we come back tomorrow and hike? Or does everyone want to continue on Route 66 and make our way closer to California?"

Bobby said he'd like to go back to the Grand Canyon if they could ride the burros. Sam said he'd like to go back if they could do the Skywalk. Annie and the triplets all voted at once, "On to Route 66!" Mommy said her vote counted the most and she didn't want to hike with the babies. "My vote is for Route 66, too," she said.

Daddy laughed and said, "Well, that's settled! It's on to Route 66 in the morning." No one was disappointed.

After the adventure-packed day, it wasn't long before the chugging of the train put all the Mouse children to sleep. When the train pulled into the Williams Depot, Annie jumped awake. Wiping the sleep out of her eyes, she startled the others awake when she asked in a loud voice, "Where ARE we?"

One by one, the others all woke up, laughing at Annie's confusion. Daddy asked, "Don't you remember getting on the train to go back to Williams?" Annie shook her head, rubbed her eyes a few more times, and startled them all again when she shouted, "I remember now! We just visited the Grand Canyon! Where to next?"

Mommy answered with a question of her own, "How about bed? I'm exhausted!"

But, none of the children were! They answered with one big, "NO!" to Mommy's question. They'd all just had a nap!

Daddy said, "Well, we do need to have dinner. Let's go to that diner with the tables outside. Remember the one that was playing the music last night?"

After a short walk to the diner they were quickly seated at an outdoor table. Bobby was the first to see the cowboys in the street. "Look! It's another Wild West show! We can watch it right from here!"

This time Annie wasn't afraid at all! Bobby and Sam thought this show was more exciting than the one from the night before. They even laughed when the sheriff came to break things up!

When the triplets began falling asleep into their milkshakes, Daddy decided it was time to go back to the hotel. This time, no one argued.

Chapter Twenty:

More to Arizona than the Grand Canyon!

The sounds from the train station woke Annie up early the next morning. As usual, Annie was the first to get up and couldn't control her excitement! "Get up, everyone!" she shouted. "There's still so much to see!"

This time, no one had to encourage the other children to get up and get ready. They all jumped out of bed quickly, even Jenny! They were all eager to see what other adventures were waiting for them along the rest of Arizona Route 66.

The sun was beginning to rise as they loaded up the car. Annie said she'd never seen such a beautiful sunrise before. Jenny said she wasn't sure she'd ever seen the sun rise before! Everyone laughed because they knew it was true; Jenny hated to get up in the morning! But even she thought this sunrise was amazing.

As Daddy eased the car out of the parking lot, he said, "No one seems to notice what's all around them anymore. Just like back in Flagstaff, when that young man walked off the curb. He was so busy on his phone, he didn't even realize that I almost hit him!"

Mommy added, "With all the technology we have, we don't take enough time to appreciate what's right in front of us."

As the tires thump-thump-thumped down old Route 66, Annie thought about the things Mommy and Daddy just said. How many things were right in front of her that she didn't take the time to notice? She and Jenny were always getting on each other's nerves, but it was Jenny who stood up for her at the bus stop when some big kids were pushing her. While she hated the way Sam always teased her, he was the one who carried her into the house when she fell off her bike and made sure she was okay. And even though she hated when Mommy yelled, she knew how much Mommy loved them. She loved the special cakes Mommy made for special occasions and how Mommy would read them a bedtime story every night before tucking them all into bed. She wondered if all mothers did that.

Annie stayed lost in her thoughts, thinking about all the things she hadn't taken the time to notice until Mommy startled her back to noticing what was right in front of her! Mommy sounded excited, while saying, "Look! Oh this looks like it's going to be fun!"

Daddy read the sign for the town they were about to enter, "Welcome to Seligman Birthplace of Historic Route 66."

Sam said, "Isn't this the town that has the barber shop- the one the guy owned who wouldn't let Route 66 die after the interstate passed them by?"

Daddy answered, "Yep, this is it! I'll drive up and down the street and then we'll decide where we'll stop."

Annie began to take notice of everything around her while Mommy read the signs as they passed. There was a restaurant called, "Roadkill Café," a General Store, another jail, and lots of shops and diners.

Bobby was the first to shout, "There IT is! There's the Barber Shop!"

Daddy knew that was someplace they HAD to stop, so he pulled the car over. There was so much to look at: a crazy car, Burma Shave signs, the Barber Shop pole. Everyone was squealing and pointing excitedly. Once they got inside, Angel Delgadillo greeted them. Daddy asked if he could get his hair cut, but the barber just laughed and said he didn't do that anymore, the shop was now a Route 66 Visitor's Center, but, he told them, "You can all have a seat in my barber's chair and I'll take your pictures." Annie was VERY excited about that.

When they were leaving, Angel told them to make sure to stop at the Sno Cap Drive-In. Daddy asked where it was and Angel told him he couldn't miss it!

The first thing they noticed was the crazy car parked in front. Then there were signs everywhere. When Mommy tried to open the door to go inside, there were door handles on each side! Sam said, "The guidebook said these owners were known for practical jokes!" Annie was very confused. But not too confused to enjoy her french fries!

The whole family loved Seligman, even Jenny. They spent all day, walking up and down the street, exploring the Territorial Jail, shopping in the General Store to restock their cooler and snack bag, and looking in all of the souvenir shops. After a long and exciting day, they finally stopped to have their dinner at the Roadkill Café before finding a place to stay for the night.

After getting back on the road the next morning Mommy, who was taking a turn driving, said, "I don't think we should make any more stops until we get to California."

Daddy agreed, "We've already seen so much in Arizona; there can't be that much left to see anyway."

Annie added, "Yeah, let's hurry to California!"

Jenny said, "I'm tired. I'm going to go back to sleep. Don't bother me about stopping anywhere."

They were entering Valentine when Bobby yelled, "Hey! Look at that truck! The one that says 'Wild' on the side!"

Sam added, "Yeah! Look! It has a tiger and lion coming out the top, too!"

Jenny quickly jumped up to take a look. Mommy said, "Well, I guess we were wrong; it looks like there's still a lot to see in Arizona!"

Even though they were eager to get to California, the Mouse

family couldn't resist stopping at the Keepers of the Wild in Valentine.

The children were all very excited about seeing the animals. Daddy instructed them to quiet down while he was making his donation for the tickets. As he handed the money to the clerk he apologized for the children, saying, "My kids get really excited about going to a zoo!"

Handing them a map, the clerk said, "This isn't a zoo. It's an animal rescue center. We take in animals that have been abandoned or neglected. Sometimes they were pets that got too big for the owners to handle and they don't know what to do with them. We provide them with a permanent home in a more natural habitat here, through the donations of visitors-- like you!"

Bobby said, "So- we're just going to see cats and dogs?"

"Not according to this map," Daddy answered.

"Follow me. I think it's still going to look a lot like a zoo to us."

The children excitedly followed Daddy and Mommy out the door and along the path.

When they got to the section with lions, Annie asked, "You mean people actually had LIONS for pets?!"

Bobby said, "Did you see the ELEPHANTS over here?"

Sam asked, "Could we go see the rattlesnakes?"

Jenny whined, "No! That won't turn out well!" Then she asked Daddy if they could have a giraffe for a pet.

Sam said, "That's stupid! Where would we put it?"

When Daddy gave them that look that told them they were about to get into trouble, Jenny whispered, "I was just joking. Geesh!"

Mommy and Daddy had a hard time keeping up with the older kids as they raced excitedly from one exhibit to the next. They were hot, tired and thirsty by the time they finished exploring all of the habitats.

As they piled back into the car, Sam asked, "Where's our next stop?"

"I'll know when we get there," Daddy jokingly replied.

He didn't have to wait long to find out where they would stop next. "That looks like it might be a fun stop," Mommy whispered to Daddy while pointing towards an old bus that advertised the Hackberry General Store.

"What would be a fun stop?" Sally asked.

Annie chimed in, "Fun stop? Did someone say fun stop?"

Daddy said, "I guess we'll stop at the Hackberry General Store- IF it's still in business. You never know on Route 66!"

The first thing Daddy saw as they approached the General Store was the Corvette parked in front. "Yep, we are definitely stopping here," he said excitedly.

Mommy said, "I'm not sure if it's opened or not, but there sure is a lot to see outside." She began reading the Burma Shave signs to the children.

Bobby added, "Look! There are people coming out of the building! It IS open. Can we go inside?"

Daddy agreed saying, "I'd like to learn a little more about this building. Let's go in and see what we could find out!"

Once inside, they learned that the famous Route 66 artist, Bob Waldmire, used to own the Hackberry General Store.

There was a lot to see inside the store. Annie pointed to the juke box and said, "I know what that is!"

Annie tugged on Daddy's arm, "Daddy, could we get something to drink now? I'm really hot and thirsty!"

Daddy agreed and quickly paid for some ice cold drinks for everyone and hurried the children outside to enjoy them. "You could sip on your drinks while we finish looking around," Daddy suggested. He pointed out the old gas pumps, "It's too bad they don't still sell gas, too. I'd love to fill up the old car with one of these!"

Mommy replied, "I'd love if the price of gas was the same as it was back then, too!"

Sam ran from one old car to the next, shouting, "Daddy! Did you see THIS one?"

When their drinks were finished, Daddy and Mommy instructed the children to get back into their seats so they could continue down Route 66.

The car continued to thumpity thump along the road, putting the little ones to sleep. Annie was careful to only look forward instead of out the sides. She was having too much fun and didn't want to get car sick again!

Daddy didn't stop the car again until they entered Kingman. Mommy said, "Wow! It looks like there's a lot to see in Kingman! We won't be able to see it all. Why don't you drive up and down Route 66 and we'll pick out a few places we'd like to stop or we'll never make it to Cousins Mary and Bob's house!"

Daddy thought that sounded like a great idea. After cruising through town once, Bobby pointed to the Powerhouse Visitor's Center an Route 66 Museum, saying, "That looks like a good stop."

Everyone agreed that the Route 66 Museum would be a good stop. There, they learned that the building was built in 1909 and used to supply electric power to the mines.

Sam and Bobby were eager to race up the stairs to see more displays. But Annie looked up and couldn't believe how high up the ceiling was! It made her feel dizzy. She grabbed Daddy's hand and stayed close to his side.

There was a lot to see in the museum. Daddy wasn't quite done looking around, when the babies started to cry. Mommy said they'd "had enough" and that it was time to find some ice cream.

The suggestion of ice cream always made the children settle down. They knew they wouldn't get that treat unless they were behaving themselves!

Daddy knew exactly where he planned to take them for ice cream. The Route 66 Diner he'd passed earlier was right around the corner and sure to be a hit.

With ice cream cones in hand, their next stop was the historic shopping district. Daddy said Mommy deserved a break, so he took all the kids for a walk while she went on what he called another "shop-o-rama." Annie stood staring into the window of the bookstore. She wished she could go in, but she knew she couldn't take her ice cream in the store. It had already begun dripping down her hands.

Mommy gasped when she rejoined them. "Daddy! Just LOOK at the children!"

Daddy had been so busy making sure the children stayed together, he hadn't noticed that ice cream was everywhere! It had melted quickly in the heat and all of the children seemed to be wearing more ice cream than they'd eaten.

"We've got to get these kids into a shower. Looks like it's time to check into a motel for the night," Daddy laughed.

Sam said he'd read about the Historic Brunswick Hotel that they'd passed earlier. "Maybe we could try there? I thought it looked kinda cool as we drove past it."

Bobby added, "Yeah, I read about it, too. It's supposed to be haunted."

Jenny squealed, "Oh! That sounds like fun! Can we stay there?"

Annie stood there, shaking her head. She didn't think she wanted to stay in a haunted hotel.

Daddy said, "Well, at the Powerhouse Visitor's Center, they said it was closed right now, so we'll have to find someplace else."

It didn't take Daddy long to find a place to stay. Once they saw the flashing neon Route 66 sign, they knew that was the place for them!

After Mommy had the sticky children all cleaned up and settled in for the night, Daddy said it was time to talk about the rest of the trip.

Even though the other children were asleep, Annie, while pretending to be asleep, eagerly listened as Daddy and Mommy talked. She couldn't wait to hear what they would be seeing next.

Daddy said, "I wanted to see all of Route 66, but we've been gone a long time already, and we still haven't visited with Mary and Bob. I don't think we're going to be able to make it all the way to the end of the route. Will you be upset if we don't?"

Mommy replied, "I've been a little worried about our time, too. There was so much we wanted to see in Arizona. I never expected it to take this long to get through one state! If I have to make a choice, visiting Mary and Bob is more important than making it to the end of the route. I just don't see how we could do both."

Annie listened with disappointment. But she had to admit, she was getting a little homesick, too. She really missed her friend, Molly Mole.

Daddy added, "I'm glad you're not upset. "

Mommy replied, "This trip has been wonderful so far! And the children have never been so well behaved! How could I be upset?"

Annie never heard the rest of the conversation. She had drifted off to sleep and began dreaming about children who had turned into ice cream cones.

Mommy and Daddy were startled by the giggles coming from the sleeping Annie. Daddy said, "Whatever it is, it looks like she's happy about something!"

Chapter Twenty-One:
Burros!

Early the next morning, Daddy announced that it was time to pack up and start the last leg of their journey. "Have we got a fun day planned for you kids today!"

That was enough to get them all up and scrambling to get ready. Sam and Bobby were pretty sure they knew what was in store. They had been looking through the guidebook before going to sleep. They looked at each other and said, "Oatman!"

Getting in the driver's seat, Mommy said, "You'll just have to wait and see!"

The children were all talking excitedly about the day's adventure when Mommy said, "This road is getting kind of narrow and windy. I'm going to have to concentrate on driving, so I need all of you to be very quiet."

Daddy added, "You don't want to miss this scenery, kids! It looks like we're on top of the world here!"

Annie couldn't believe how narrow the road was in places. She could see the look of concern on Mommy's face. Daddy kept saying, "You're doing fine. Just take it slow and easy."

They passed by Cool Springs, another Route 66 Museum and gift shop. Daddy said that it looked like it would be a "cool" place to stop. "Too bad it's so early in the morning and not open yet. I hope it's open on the way home!"

Sam pointed to the sign for Sitgreaves Pass and said, "Look! We're 3550 feet high!"

Mommy looked even more concerned and continued to grip the steering wheel tightly. She made each bend and curve without any trouble. Suddenly, she slammed on the brakes. There, right in front of the car, were wild burros on the roadway. They didn't seem to be in any hurry to get out of the car's way, either!

This sent the children into fits of giggles. Mommy relaxed her grip on the steering wheel. As she inched the car forward she said, "I guess I'll just follow the burros into town!"

Once in the historic gold mining town she pulled into the first parking place she could find, relieved to be done driving. She looked at Daddy and joked, "I sure picked a fine time to volunteer to drive, didn't I?"

Annie squealed, "Look! There are more burros going into that store over there."

Everyone looked in the direction Annie was pointing. There were, indeed, burros entering the shop. Jenny said, "I guess they like to go shopping."

Daddy said, "What are we waiting for? Let's get out and explore Oatman! It looks just like a wild west town!"

Everyone scrambled to get out of the car. Immediately, they saw signs posted that instructed them not to feed the burros. Bobby said, "That's odd. Our guidebook said that you could feed the burros with carrots that you buy in the stores."

Mommy said, "Something must have happened. Maybe someone got bit."

Daddy added, "They are wild animals. I don't think it would be a good idea to feed them, anyway!"

Annie didn't think she wanted to get close enough to feed them.

Sam pointed, "Look over there! Maybe now that no one is feeding them carrots, they want ice cream!"

It looked like the burros had lined up at an ice cream counter waiting their turn to buy ice cream! There were burros everywhere!

Mommy made everyone laugh when she said, "Remember yesterday? No Mouse children will be getting ice cream now! The burros would be licking you all clean!"

They entered the Oatman Hotel and gasped when they saw the walls covered in dollar bills. Annie asked, "Daddy, why do they put money on the WALLS?"

A clerk, who overheard Annie's question, told the family that people from all over the world sign their names on the bills and tack them to the walls.

"Let's go visit all the other shops and come back here to eat lunch," Mommy suggested.

"You won't want to miss the Wild West Shootout show after lunch," the clerk added.

Sam and Bobby liked that idea a lot! "Could we see the show, too, Daddy?" they asked.

"Only if you behave yourselves while Mommy is shopping," Daddy answered.

All the kids shouted at once, "We'll be good, Daddy! Promise!"

The shops were close together and Mommy wanted to visit ALL of them. In each shop they learned something new.

They learned that in the early 1900s Oatman was one of the biggest producers of gold in Arizona. The miners used the burros to carry loads. The mines closed during World War II when the government needed the miners for other things and the burros were set free. Wild burros continue to roam Oatman and the surrounding areas today.

They also learned that only a few years earlier people were allowed to feed the burros, but it's now discouraged. Since wild animals do bite and kick, the Bureau of Land Management determined that it isn't safe for people to feed them and it's not healthy for the burros to be eating so much.

The children had so much fun strolling through the shops, learning new things while talking to the shop owners, and seeing interesting things that no one even had to remind them to behave. The time went so fast that Annie was surprised when Daddy said it was time to go have lunch.

Annie had never eaten anywhere that had money all over the walls before. Sam and Bobby tried to see if they could count the money before their food came, but they kept losing their place. They were still at it when their food arrived, but Daddy reminded them they didn't want to miss the Wild West show.

With meals finished, they went outside to watch the "showdown."

This time Annie wasn't afraid since she knew it was just a show. Even though she didn't get as excited as her brothers did, she found herself enjoying the show.

After the Wild West show Daddy said it was time to finish driving through Arizona and head to Cousins Mary and Bob's house.

Chapter Twenty-Two:
California: A Visit with Cousins Mary and Bob

As they approached California, Daddy saw what looked like a border patrol check point of some kind that he had no choice but to enter. Mommy asked Daddy if maybe he made a mistake and was entering Mexico instead of California. Daddy felt very confused as he followed the line of traffic into the area.

When a man in uniform came over to the car, Daddy rolled the window down. The uniformed man, a border guard, said, "Sir, do you have any fruits or vegetables in your car?"

Daddy thought it was a joke and began to laugh. The Mouse children began to giggle, too. The uniformed man did NOT laugh. Daddy quickly got serious and answered, "Yes, I believe we have a few apples in our cooler."

The guard instructed Daddy to get out of the car and show him the apples. Confused, Daddy went to the back of the car where Annie was sitting and opened the cooler lid to show the apples. The guard told Daddy he would have to keep them because travelers are not permitted to bring fruits and vegetables into the state of California.

Annie was listening and wondered if they were going to be taken to jail! She didn't want to go to jail, especially after seeing what the jails looked like across Route 66. She began to cry. The guard asked Annie why she was crying. Annie gulped and asked, "Are you taking us to jail because we have some apples?"

It was the man's turn to laugh. He replied, "No, you're not going to jail. I'm sorry I frightened you. You see, we grow fruits and vegetables in California and when people bring in their own from outside of the state they might have bugs on them that could harm our crops. That's why we don't allow fruits and vegetables to come in from outside of California."

They were all relieved to learn they weren't in any trouble. After the guard took their apples, he allowed them to continue into California. As they drove away, Mommy said she couldn't believe they had food taken away from them! Daddy replied that he wasn't going to worry about that; he was eager to see California!

In the excitement of the border patrol stop, Annie had almost forgotten where they were! She blurted, "Yes! California! We're finally here!"

The rest of the children all started bouncing and shouting, "California! California!" until Daddy had to pull the car over to settle them down.

Daddy asked sternly, while trying not to laugh, "Do you want me to turn around and go home now?"

By the time he finished the question, he was giggling as much as they were. Everyone knew Daddy wasn't going to go home without

visiting Cousins Mary and Bob since they were now so close.

Finally Daddy said, "I'm just as excited about being in California as you are! I can't believe we made it all across the country! But I have to be able to concentrate on driving, so you have to settle down."

Once the children were settled, Daddy continued driving.

Mommy said their last stop before arriving at her relatives would be in Needles. They stopped to take pictures around the Conestoga wagon that welcomes visitors into the town. Annie commented that the palm trees looked different than she had expected them to look; they were much bigger and taller.

Before continuing to Cousins Mary and Bob's house, Daddy drove through the town to find the El Garces hotel that was being restored and would one day be as beautiful as La Posada. Annie took a few more pictures before Mommy said they should be going.

Annie closed her eyes and sat back in her seat. She began thinking about all of their adventures that they would share with their relatives. She couldn't wait to show all of her pictures! What would she tell them about first? Would it be the murals or Henry's Rabbit Ranch, or The Blue Whale or the burros in Oatman, or...?

Mommy's announcement that they would soon be at Cousin Mary and Bob's house startled Annie back to the present.

Daddy pointed to a street sign and said, "Here it is!"

As Daddy turned onto the street, Mommy told the children to start looking for the correct house number. Daddy drove slowly down the street until Sam shouted, "There it is," while pointing to the home with palm trees in front.

As Daddy eased the car into the driveway, Mommy reminded the children to be on their best behavior while they were guests here. But as soon as Daddy parked the car and everyone got out, Mary and Bob came out of the house and everyone went running.

Annie thought she was going to be squished as everyone hugged at once! It seemed like everyone was talking at once, too, while introductions were being made.

Annie tugged on Mommy's skirt and whispered, "I really hafta go to the bathroom, Mommy!" Annie did not want to have an accident, but she couldn't just walk into the house by herself!

Cousin Mary laughed, "Where are my manners? You all must need to freshen up and find the bathrooms. Let me show you to your rooms before dinner."

Cousin Bob said he hoped they were hungry because dinner was almost ready.

Mommy hurried the children along, instructing them to quickly use the bathroom and wash their hands. "I think our hosts have waited on us long enough today. I'm sure they want to eat their dinner!"

As they made their way to the backyard, the smell coming from the grill made Annie realize how hungry she was!

This was the start of the Mouse family's week-long pattern of sitting around the large backyard picnic table, eating and talking. Mommy said she never realized Cousin Bob was such a gourmet chef! Daddy said if they kept eating like this they wouldn't all fit in the car when it was time to leave!

"I guess we'll have to leave a few of the kids here if that happens," Daddy joked.

Annie decided she would be careful not to eat too much- just in case Daddy WASN'T joking! As much as she was enjoying her visit in California, she was beginning to miss home.

With dinner over, Mommy announced that she had forgotten to bring in a few items from the car. She asked Annie and Bobby to come with her to help carry the packages. Annie was confused for a minute and then she remembered the special presents they had purchased.

When they returned from the car, Annie proudly presented Mary with the vase and Bobby gave the chess set to Bob. Annie grinned from ear to ear when she saw Mary's expression. She exclaimed, "OH! This is beautiful! I have wanted a horse hair pottery vase for a long time."

"I'm surprised you know what it is. I had never heard of horse hair pottery until Annie noticed a few items," Mommy offered.

Annie beamed, "I'm glad you like it. I picked it out."

Mary kissed her on the cheek and said, "Well, Annie, you have very good tastes in vases. I have admired them, but didn't want to splurge on myself. Now I'm glad I didn't buy one. It is so much more special coming as a gift."

They turned their attention to Bob, who was opening the chess set. Bob was equally pleased with his gift. "I haven't played chess in quite some time. This is a beautiful set. Does anyone want to play with me?"

"I'd like to play with you, but I've never played before. You'd have to teach me how," Bobby responded.

Bob said, "We'll have our first game tomorrow, right after breakfast. It's getting a little late to start now."

Mommy added, "It's been a long day. I think we should help Mary and Bob clean up the kitchen and then get ready for bed."

Each morning after breakfast, Bob played a game of chess with Bobby, teaching him more with each game, while the others watched. After lunch, he played another game with Sam or Daddy.

Each night after dinner, Annie shared a different state's photographs with Mary and Bob. They eagerly looked through Annie's pictures as the Mouse family shared their cross-country adventures.

Bob was pleased to discover they'd stopped at one of his favorite pizza places in the country. "Boy, this is making me want to drive to Joplin just to get some of Woody's pizza!"

Mary suggested they do a road trip soon. "Looking at all of your pictures makes me want to discover Route 66 all over again! There's so much that I never saw or paid attention to when we made the trip," she added.

The week flew by! When it was time to leave, Daddy said they'd have to take the quick route back home. They'd already been gone from home longer than they had expected.

Bob said, "You'll have to come back next year."

Mary added, "You know you are welcome any time!"

Daddy said, "I'm thinking maybe next year we'll fly to Los Angeles and rent a car and do Route 66 from west to east. There's so much we wanted to see that we had to pass by on our way here."

Bob said, "You can never see all of Route 66 in one trip."

As they hugged each other goodbye, Mary asked, "So, we can count on seeing you next year, then?"

While loading the children back in the car, Mommy answered, "I hope so, I can't wait!"

Daddy drove slowly away while the children continued blowing kisses and waving goodbye.

As soon as Cousins Mary and Bob were out of sight, Annie

pulled her notebook out. She began making a list of all the places she hoped they'd see next year. She filled page after page in her notebook as she worked on the list every day until they got home.

As the car pulled into their driveway, Annie said, "Daddy, I think we have to take a Route 66 trip every year until I graduate from high school to see everything I still want to see!"

"Annie, I think that's a great idea," Daddy replied.

Grinning, Mommy added, "I guess Gary Turner was right - by the time you get home from your first trip, you'll already be planning the next one."

Daddy parked the car amidst the children's clapping and cheers.

Resources

Hinckley, Jim. (2012). The Route 66 Encyclopedia. Voyageur Press.

McClanahan, Jerry. (2008). Route 66: EZ66 Guide for Travelers: Second edition. National Historic Route 66 Federation.

National Historic Route 66 Federation. (2008.) Route 66 Dining & Lodging Guide.

Ross, Jim; & McClanahan, Jerry. (2005). Here It Is! The Route 66 Map Series. Ghost Town Press.

Snyder, Tom. (2000). Route 66: Traveler's Guide and Roadside Companion. St. Martin's Griffin.

Wallis, Michael. (2001). Route 66: The Mother Road 75th Anniversary Edition. St. Martin's Griffin.

Wickline, David. (2006). Images of 66: An Interactive Photographic Journey along the Length of the Mother Road. Roadhouse 66, LLC.

Acknowledgments

Cadillac Ranch ©1974 ANT FARM
Cadillac is a registered trademark of General Motors Corporation.

DQ is a registered trademark of The American Dairy Queen Corporation, which is a subsidiary of Berkshire Hathaway, Inc.

Fallingwater, located in Mill Run, PA, was designed by the famous architect, Frank Lloyd Wright. It is a National Historic Landmark and is maintained by the Western Pennsylvania Conservancy.

"I Love Lucy" was produced by Desilu Studios from 1951-1957.

"Jailhouse Rock" is a song written by Jerry Leiber and Mike Stoller and recorded by Elvis Presley.

"Standin' on a corner in Winslow, Arizona", is from the song, "Take it Easy", written by Jackson Browne and Glenn Frey (1972) and recorded by The Eagles.

Quotes attributed to the Mouse Family's "guide book" or "travel guide" are not actual quotes, but represent information compiled from the author's actual Route 66 trips, talking to owners of businesses along the route and from the variety of books listed under "Resources."